Hindola

Ranganath Srinivasa

Invincible Publishers

First published in India in 2017 by Invincible Publishers

ISBN: 978-93-86148-64-3

Invincible Publishers
G - 120, Sushant Lok III, Sector 57, Gurgaon-122002

Opposite Kasturba Ashram, Radaur Distt Yamuna Nagar, Haryana- 135133

Dedication

This book is dedicated in the memory of my parents
Sri. Srimushnam Srinivasa Murthy and
Smt. Rukmini

Just before the start

* * *

It was a musical programme by two sisters. It was a jugalbandhi of the Hindola and Malkauns ragaas. These two raagas have always attracted me. The Hindola composition was sweet and melodious. The Malkauns alaaps captured my mood. It was at this instant that the story of Hindola was born.

I started writing and my thoughts and feelings poured out. In the end, a romantic story replete with emotions emerged. I have always believed that human values weigh uppermost in our value system. I think I have succeeded in presenting that message.

After the completion of my novel, I approached Mr Ajay Sethia of Invincible publishers. He happily agreed to publish this novel under the banner of Invincible publications. I am very grateful to him.

Ms. Malvika has done a splendid job of editing this book. Bhavna Sharma evinced a keen interest in the story line and did the second level of editing very beautifully. I am extremely grateful to both of them.

Ms. Sneha Agarwal has designed the cover image very imaginatively. The musical waves and the notes in the backdrop of the seashore are presented very beautifully. I am extremely thankful to her.

My son Sudeep and my daughter-in-law Ruchira, staying in the U.S., evinced a lot of interest in the story line. I am very thankful to them for their moral support and encouragement.

My daughter, Suman Jayathirtha, is a great source of help and encouragement. My daughter was the first reader of this novel in its manuscript stage. She helped me sending the e-mails and other related online works. I am very thankful to her.

I am extremely grateful to my wife Indumathi for following the development of the story and tolerating my erratic schedule of work and leisure hours.

I feel confident that this novel will be well received by all book lovers happily.

Chapter 1

* * *

It was a night journey by bus. He was heading towards Udupi. The mountainous terrain seemed endless. It was dark and drizzling. The lights inside the bus were lit and the bus came to a halt. The passenger seated next to him dragged him into a conversation. He was in no mood to talk. He was proceeding towards Udupi where his wife's parents were living. He was travelling alone this time.

"Are you going to Udupi for the first time?" the co-passenger asked him.

"Oh! No. I have come here a number of times. My wife's parents stay here."

"I am Rao, Govinda Rao. I am a doctor by profession. I had come to Bangalore for a seminar. Tell me something about you?"

"I am Aloknath Vyasathirtha. I teach English in a college in Bangalore."

"Alok, a beautiful name. Isn't, it?.. What brings you to Udupi, … alone?".

"I am an English teacher by profession. Writing is my hobby. I published my first novel. It was a moderate success in the literary business. I thought I would have to do more research before I start writing the second novel."

"But why Udupi"?

"My wife is busy with the children; in making them study, helping them to prepare for the examination, things of that sort, you know. My summer vacation is about to start. My father-in-law fell down and has fractured his leg. He needs a support. Somebody, who can lift him and try to support him and make him walk, help him to the toilet etc. My wife wanted to appoint a male nurse. Since I was free, I offered to help."

"It is very nice of you to show so much concern in your wife's parents. These days, people prefer to keep their parents in old age homes."

As the bus started moving, both of them slept.

The next morning they landed in Udupi. Alok managed to get a cab. He reached at his wife's house. As he was about to knock the door, he heard a melodious humming voice from inside. It was a beautiful 'alaap'. He stood there motionless, spellbound by the melody of the voice.. The alaap was divine. After a few minutes, he knocked the door.

She came near the door inside the house.

"Please do come in. Is it Alok?"

"Yes. Who are you? Where are Vasundhara's parents.?"

"They will be here shortly. They have gone out for an early morning walk....

...See they have already come."

An aged couple got down from a luxurious car.

"Hey! Alok. Thanks for coming. It is a big help to me." Alok's father- in- law Krishna greeted Alok very warmly."

"How are you Alok? How is Vasundhara? How are the children?"

Vasundhara's mother Rukmini was very happy to see her son-in-law.

"All are fine."

Alok got freshened up in the room he usually stayed. This room is more luxurious than his room in Bangalore. Krishna was an influential person in Udupi. He was quite affluent. Krishna's efforts in getting Alok moved to Udupi were futile. Nevertheless, Alok liked Udupi because this house was a huge one in the middle of a small town. The atmosphere was calm. Nature was in its purest form; tranquil and serene. The sea was close to the house. He could walk to the seashore in the evenings.

The next evening Alok and his father-in-law were seated outside, in the lawn in two chairs.

"So, how is your literary activity coming along?" Krishna asked.

"My first novel didn't do quite well as you know. I am trying to work on an interesting story. I am trying to do some research. I want to choose a new place, different types of characters, different situations. A particular raaga is haunting me. I want my story to revolve round it."

"You mean a musician's story?"

"Oh no. I want an undercurrent of a musical raaga to flow throughout the novel and that should be based on the emotions that this raga can manifest. So I want to study about this 'raaga' in a greater depth. I want to do some research on this. By the way, who is that girl in the house."

"That is Revathi. She helps us in the mornings. She prepares breakfast for us in the morning. Vasundhara's mother was very proud of her fitness. Nowadays, she gets frequent knee pain and can't strain herself. The doctor attending to her suggested this arrangement. Because we can't expect Vasundhara to be present here all the time. ..

....But you have substituted her. It is very nice of you."

"Who is the doctor attending to you?"

"Dr. Kalyani. I would like to call her my sister. She herself comes to our house. She talks to us very affectionately.

By the way, Dr. Kalyani is a great musician herself. About fifteen years ago, she used to give musical concerts. She has a melodious voice. She was attracted by this girl Revathi's voice and offered to keep her in her house. Revathi was undergoing a Nurse training then. But, she had discontinued her studies due to financial problems. Dr. Kalyani persuaded her to complete her training. She is a nurse working in Manipal hospital

But the girl seems to be more interested in music. I think you should meet Dr. Kalyani. She may be helpful in your research."

"That is interesting. I should meet Dr. Kalyani."

"I will call Dr. Kalyani and tell her that you will be meeting her.

"The next morning, Alok was ready, dressed up neatly in his informal attire. He was waiting for Revathi to finish her work.

"Come, sir . We will go to Madam's house. She will be waiting for you".

"Please call me Alok. Please don't call me sir."

"That is very nice of you Alok. I simply love this name."

They walked all through. They walked on the sands of the sea shore. There was greenery on one side and the sea on the other side: it was the sea permeating endlessly with the clear blue water, sometimes changing its colour to greener shades. Revathi was walking along with him holding the handle of her cycle.

"Do you know which raaga you were humming when I entered?" Alok asked her.

"The 'alaap' is so melodious and I keep humming it very frequently. That is Malkauns."

"Can you sing songs based on Hindola?"

"Of course, I can. That is my most favourite raaga."

"What do you know about that raaga?".

"That question, you have to ask madam, of course."

Dr Kalyani led her guest inside the drawing room of her huge beautiful house. The drawing room was very tastefully decorated with some beautiful paintings, some rare antiques and artistic objects.

Revathi went out to fetch some provisions and vegetables.

"These paintings are awesome Dr. Kalyani. I presume that these are your paintings."

"Painting is my hobby. Most of my time is spent in the hospital and college. I like teaching. My time in the house is spent in singing, listening and sometimes painting".

"I had the chance of listening to your student Revathi's 'alaap' as soon as I entered the house. She has a melodious voice"

"She truly has a very sweet voice. She wanted to become a doctor. But her guardians could not afford to pay the fees. She had joined the Nursing course when I met her. She had to discontinue that course. But I persuaded her to complete the training. She is a qualified nurse and works in our hospital. Her guardians were more interested in getting her married. The husband loves her, but is never available to her. He is a cab driver. Recently, she lost her five-year-old-son. The boy was playing in the beach. She was sitting absent-minded on the sands of the beach. The child's dead body was the only thing they could recover the next morning. She was in a state of mental trauma that had driven her into depression. I managed to bring her home, divert her attention to music. She has a melodious voice."

"Oh my God. That is the reason why that 'alaap' was so soulful."

"She sings the Hindola very beautifully. You should listen to her 'devara naamaas' (devotional songs).

By the way, you wanted some help for your next novel from me. Krishna rang me up and requested me to help you.

Tell me what can I do for you".

"The raaga Hindola has fascinated me very much. I don't want the musicology part of it, the notes, the missing notes, aarohana, the avarohana etc. I just want you to tell me something about the mood it can create, the emotions it can manifest."

"Hindola is a very beautiful raaga on the pentatonic scale. It does not make use of the rishabha and the panchama. It is a very soothing sweet raaga used generally to carry the feelings of melancholy, devotion and submission. When sung, it produces a feeling of pathos, a sweetness , a feeling that keeps you haunting. It is mesmerizing. It is hypnotic. I like " Saamagaana lolane", "Saamajavaragamana", sung by eminent musicians like Bombay Jaayashree. I like a beautiful kannada song " Bhameya nodalu taa banda brundaavanadinda", "Chandramukhi , PraNasaKhi" .etc. I like " Marghali poove" a Tamil song. I like " Rajahamsame" a Malayaalam song sung by Chitra. Some of these haunt me to such an extent that I can forget that I am alone here."

"Very true. This raaga haunts me for its sweetness."

"So, how are things at Bangalore….? A vibrant city"

"It is fine. But you can't find this tranquility or serenity there. Life is very mechanical in Bangalore"

'Hmm" ..Dr. Kalyani seemed to agree with Alok's view.

"Okay. I will take your leave. It is lunch time. I don't want to keep my parents waiting."

He bade good bye and returned home.

Krishna asked him, "How did you find Kalyani."

"Oh! She is fabulous. She is graceful and talks very nicely. May be, I would be meeting her on a few more occasions"

The whole night Alok was thinking about Revathi's life. She appeared to be more beautiful as he thought about her. How could life be so cruel? Her child's death had driven her to depression. The power of music has brought hope in her life. She has such a sweet voice. The beautiful malkauns alaap was reverberating in his ears. He dreamt of sitting with her on the beach and she singing that. He decided to ask her this favour.

The next morning Revathi was there. She appeared like an angel. He asked her,

"Can we go together and spend sometime in the evening in the beach?"

"Why?" she quipped.

"I want you to sing that Malkauns raaga just for me."

"I can give you the recorded version. I will give you the pendrive."

"Is it your voice?" he asked her.

"No. it is sung by two sisters. One sings in Hindola. The other sings in Malkauns. Somehow the alaap sung by the younger sister captured me. I recorded it. Played it over and over."

"I think I am in just love with that raaga and because of that I have fallen in love with you."

"Hey. Be careful. You are a married man with two children. I am a married woman just recovering from the loss of my son after a depression. To be honest, I did get such feelings with you. But I have controlled my emotions".

"Sorry. If I have hurt your feelings. I do respect your feelings. But it just came out. I am a little extrovert."

"Very nice of you. We will remain good friends. We will keep our relations to just that. We will not carry this any further."

"Surely".

Chapter 2

* * *

Alok:

I was thinking all alone. No doubt I talked as if I was a great person, restrained and sacred. But, I am just not able to forget that beautiful face, the innocence in her beauty, her sweet resonant voice, the way she utters my name. For once, I realized that my name is so beautiful. The singing part. Oh! There is some divinity in her voice. There is a power of attraction in that voice.

The cell phone was ringing . I came down to the Earth. It was my wife Vasundhara.

"I called up to tell you that the examinations of your children are going to start on Monday. Please talk to them and cheer them up. That would go a long way to boost their performance."

"Sure. How are you dear?"

"I am alright. Talk to your children."

"Hi children! All the best for your exams. Do well. Just follow Mummy's advice."

"Thank you appa. When are you coming?"

"Soon."

This talk over the phone relieved my heart. While

thinking about Revathi, I was oscillating between the extreme emotions of fearlessness and responsibility. I cannot, of course, stop thinking about these emotions.

That evening I walked along the beach. The sea waves were high. The waves appeared to carry in all my emotions. I kept looking through the sea. The sun appeared to slowly sink into the sea. The sea was tranquil sometimes and suddenly a huge wave appeared with a thundering sound. The song of the sea when it was calm, peaceful was really melodious and divine. I thought of a beautiful name Samudra geethe ("The song of the sea").

I was thinking of my early schooling, my mother a pragmatic fighter, my father an idealist, who always put society above his family. How the way they struggled in life to make our home and to bring us up. My mentor, my English teacher Dr Rao, Mangala, my Kannada teacher, walked through in my mind. The song glorifying the woman, sang by her in a college function was playing in my mind. It sent fresh waves down the memory lane. As the sea waves were dancing, I thought of the memories that I had captured. Those songs, inter-section cricket matches, functions, seminars, I don't think I will ever get them back.

I cannot forget my English poetry classes conducted by Professor Dr. Rao who talked eloquently on romantic age poetry. The way he gave the readings of the beautiful poems by Keats, Byron, Coleridge was amazing and had a profound effect in my growth as an English teacher. Some of these poems, even today keep lingering in my ears. I started emulating him slowly without my knowledge. When I became an English teacher, I became popular both inside the class room and outside. I had some favourite students. Vasundhara, a student of mine was a very obedient girl. She was a student from the science section. All the students had to study English. I was teaching poetry. Many of them didn't like to attend English classes. But most of the times, I went on explaining some of the poems of romantic age. I used to tell them the circumstances under which the romantic age started. My lecture used to generally run in this manner.

"Romanticism was fuelled by the French revolution. It was a reaction to the scientific rationalism and classicism of the age of enlightenment. It emphasized the importance of individual imagination and creativity."

Vasundhara used to listen to me with rapt attention. We became friendly, loved each other and got married. She was a very devoted wife. She had come from an aristocratic family and I had my own doubts about her adapting to my style of living. I frankly told her that I come from a lower middle class family and that I cannot afford to meet all her requirements. But, she just wanted to marry me. Her parents tried to get me to Udupi, so that Vasundhara could continue to live in her luxurious way. I didn't like the idea of being a parasite. Vasundhara made it clear that she would be living the way she chose to live. She even refused her parents' offer to buy us a house in Bangalore. We raised a happy family with two children Adithya and Apoorva. It was at this juncture that my father-in-law fractured his leg. Since he was highly diabetic, things got worse and he became partially mobile. Vasundhara stayed for some time to look after her father, but had to come back because of our family commitments.

Revathi:

It was certainly easy for me to talk very realistically. But his deep voice was resonant, charged with emotions. I could make out his struggle to produce a real good story. He does have that ability. He is articulate. He appears to be sincere in his tone. Perhaps, only a man can overtly come out with such an emotional outburst to express love. To be honest, I had the same feelings. But my son Christopher's death has shaken me. It appeared as if a part of my body has been severed. I sat on the beach alone, gazing at the waves. The tides appear to dance to the tune of my emotions. My husband, Allan, was also suffering mentally. He appeared to be more controlled. He had the responsibility of running the family. He is the eldest of the three brothers. He has a cab which he bought on a loan. He wants to clear the loan first. So, he is a workaholic. Joseph and George are growing in a very irresponsible manner. George used to present himself as a real estate businessman. He is more interested in selling the small land we have. My mother-in-law, Gracey, is very affectionate and motherly. She is a great source of inspiration and hope. Joseph is the youngest. He is a school drop-out. He wants to be a musician. Both the brothers were only dreaming and did not do any useful work. I was in this family where each one of them is loved by the other. But nobody wants to take the responsibility of running the family. So, here I was in this family with a loving husband, who had absolutely no time for his wife. The sea was my only soul mate. I could sit there on the beach gazing at the sky in the evenings waiting for the sun to set into the ocean. When the sun disappeared, my emotions would slowly melt and evaporate making me aware of the ground realities. It was on one of these evenings, when I was in my deep pensive, thoughtful moods charged with melancholy, I met this elderly couple.

The elderly couple was gazing at the sky for a long time. The gentleman was trying to get up. The old woman was trying to help him. She lost control and skid on the sands. I saw the old woman fall and ran towards her and supported her.

"Thank you. I do not have the strength to support him. I am having giddiness," the old woman spoke to me.

"Please slowly walk with me. You can have some coffee or tea. Or wait. I will go and get it myself".

"Oh! Don't bother. It is very nice of you. Thank you

very much. You are very beautiful. What is your name?"

"Revathi... Revathi Allan. I stay close to the beach."

"You come to the beach every day?"

"Almost. I work in Manipal hospital. I am a nurse."

"Do you know Dr. Kalyani"

"Surely. She is my mentor. How do you know her?"

"She is a good friend of mine. She is our doctor also."

As we kept talking, we reached the place where the car was parked. The driver came running as soon as he saw the aged couple moving towards the car. I held Krishna's hand. The driver helped him to go get inside the car.

"Thank you very much. It was very nice talking to you. I will tell Kalyani that I met you. We will drop you. Why don't you come?"

"Thank you. I have come by my cycle."

The car drove off. I stood there for some time. The sunset seemed to completely set by now.

When I returned to my home, I was thinking about my parents. Who could they be?.

My childhood memories went back to Sr. Clara who was everything to me. The convent was my world. Fr. Desouza was our protector. He built the beautiful church and the convent. I remember my choir. The musical ensemble consisted of a group of young girls. I was the main singer. Father had selected me because my voice was considered to be very melodious. I enjoyed singing the Christmas carols, the devotional hymns and every musical activity of the church. The church ran a high school. My Kannada teacher liked me very much because I talked in a very chaste Kannada. Besides, she liked my voice. In every school function invocation was invariably done by me. She took Father's permission and took me to musical classes after school hours. By the time I finished twelfth standard examination I had reached a level, where I could perform on the stage. Father was my greatest source of strength and inspiration.

He told me once, "If you wish to pursue a medical career, work hard and get a seat in St. John's or the Christian Medical College, Vellore. I will try to get a sponsorship for you from the church. But, if you desire to pursue a career in music, you are free to do so. Either way, you will be serving the Lord."

Father paid the fee for my music classes. I never felt that I was an orphan. My teachers, my friends, everyone was fond of me.

Father had gone abroad for three months. Sr. Clara was my mother, father and was everything to me. It was during this summer that I met George, a cab driver. He was a distant relative of Father Desouza. He had come to meet Father. I was sitting inside the church compound. I was reading some novel. If I remember, it was "The Guide" written by R.K.Narayan.

The tall handsome young gentleman accosted me.

"Hey , I am Allan Desouza. Father's nephew."

"Nice to meet you Allan. I stretched my hands to shake hands with him."

He shook hands with me very warmly.

"You are very beautiful. Father said you sing very well."

"Why did Father speak to you about me?"

You were in the field. In the field of view from Father's office on the first floor, I was curious to know about you since your face appeared as if an angel had condescended".

"What else did Father say about me?"

"He said you are the leader of the choir. You stay in the convent and you are a brilliant student."

"Bye then. We will meet next time."

Allan used to come frequently and used to meet me every time. I also felt very happy in his company. We fell in love.

One day Father called me.

"Allan says he is in love with you and you also love him. Is it true?"

I was shocked and silent. I didn't expect him to move so fast. I was shivering. I could not lift my head. I was crying.

"It is alright. Sr. Clara has gone to Mangalore. She will come tonight. I will discuss with her. You can go now. You have secured a seat in the Nursing College. The church will sponsor your studies. After you finish the course, we will fix you up in a hospital. Till then you should stop thinking of all these fantasies, dreams, love Okay?"

"Yes Father. Sorry Father."

"Don't feel sorry. You have not committed any mistake. This is very natural for a girl of your age. If both of you love each other, your marriage will happen here only, but not now. After you finish your course and settle down with a job.

I have spoken to Allan also. He has promised me. He will not disturb you."

The next day Sr. Clara arrived. I was mortally scared of facing her. She came to my room and started talking.

"Revathi, when I took you in my lap, I became your mother. I am very possessive about you. I can't even imagine that you could think of these things. But, you are eighteen years old now. I request you child, not to let me down. I have imagined so many things about your future. I should see you as a famous doctor. I also imagine you making those beautiful alaaps and singing beautiful ragaas. The very thought of you leaving the church makes me feel miserable. We will make you enter the medical field. God willing, you may even become a doctor. You are a very bright child. At the moment, we are only concerned about your career and not marriage".

" Sister, I haven't done anything to let you down. He just came to me and started talking to me. We became good friends. He said he loved me".

"And you said Yes."

"Yes"

" Sister was sobbing profusely. You didn't think of me when you said yes?"

I remained silent. I was rendered speechless. For the first time, I felt how much Sister cared for me. I used to shout at her, quarrel with her, taunt her, play with her. I now realized how important she was to me. She was bigger in my mind than what I could visualize.

I just rushed towards her and hugged her firmly.

"Sister. Please forgive me. My mother deserted this world the next instant after I was born. My father deserted me. You told me that I was just ten days old when my grandfather brought me here. Who else is there for me? I promise you that I will not entertain such feelings. Hereafter, I will be just your daughter. Please don't allow anyone to adopt me. I will remain in the church".

Sr. Clara controlled her feelings. She started talking in a motherly tone.

"That is not what I meant. I want you to settle down in your life. You have beauty, intelligence and that beautiful voice. Why did the Lord not allow your mother to watch your growth?"

Sr. Clara was thinking of that early morning eighteen years ago.

She was returning from her prayer meeting. It was a good Friday, the day of crucifixion of Jesus. She was fasting and observing penance. An old man with a ten day old infant in his arms with torn and dirty clothes was standing outside the church compound.

"Come in the evening. They will distribute food in the evening. Now you have to go".

The security guard was trying to evict him from the premises.

"I have walked through a long distance. Please call

Father."

"Father will come outside only at 10 am. You wait outside."

Sr. Clara observed the security guard forcing the old man to go out.

"John, What is the matter?"

"Looks like a beggar. Wants to meet Father."

"Can you please tell me why you want to meet the Father?"

"Sister, this is my daughter's daughter. The baby is ten days old. My daughter, an eighteen year old girl was raped by some fellow. I lost my wife when my daughter was just one-year-old. I brought her up. By the time I came to know that my daughter was a pregnant, I could not even arrange for an abortion. In our village the birth of a female baby is considered to be a scorn. She was under-nutritious and very weak. The doctors in the village hospital did their best. But, they could only save this baby. I could not save my daughter. Now I am very old and cannot work. I could not throw this child to the municipality dustbin. A relative of mine suggested that I should leave this child in the convent."

"Father is very busy at the moment. You come on Monday. I will speak to the Father. Have some food. You give the baby to me."

Sr. Clara experienced a tender feeling on taking the baby in her arms. Fr. Bernard agreed to bring up the child in the church. The child was christened Reena.

The music teacher started calling her Revathi. Sr. Clara asked the music teacher:

"Why do you always call her Revathi?"

"Revathi is a raaga, generally used to sing in the praise of the God."

Sr. Clara went on lying to me that my parents were very poor and could not bring me up. Sr. Clara thought many times that she should inform me that I lost my mother soon after my birth. But, she could never do this as she thought that would make me feel very sorrowful and that would affect my career.

I was thinking about my parents. Who could they be? I sometimes thought that I was like a flowing river without knowing where it started. The fact that I was brought to the convent by my grandfather became known to me only through a senior inmate of the convent. Sister had informed Dr. Kalyani that I belonged to a poor family. But where is that family? Why did they leave me? Questions answered, some unanswered always have haunted me. These are the questions which have been left unanswered throughout my life.

Father found a sponsor to take care of my expenses in the nursing college. Simultaneously, I was doing my music classes. I completed my nursing course examination. I was appointed a nurse in Manipal hospital.

I got married to Allan. He bought a cab on a loan. We lived happily along with Gracey, my mother-in-law and my brothers-in-law. Allan shouldered a great responsibility of the family. Christopher was born two years after my marriage. I was in the seventh heavens.

Christopher was five-years-old. Allan had gone on a long tour. I was sitting on the sea shore allowing Christopher to play on the beach. Suddenly, all the people started moving away from the beach. The tides of the sea waves were very high. The winds were blowing at a very high speed. It was very difficult to stand; let alone walk. There was commotion all around. I started looking out for Christopher.

The powerful winds had pushed Christopher into the sea. He had already been drowned.

Joseph and George came running. They swam for a long time in the sea trying to find Christopher. George finally found Christopher's body and had to be pulled out by his hair against the direction of the waves and winds.

We waited for Allan. He came the next day after a long hectic drive.

We buried Christopher and conducted a funeral service.

I was shocked beyond grief. Tears didn't come out.

Gracey told me,

"I think we are cursed. I could not protect my grandson. I should not have sent him with you. Every day I used to tell him to stay at home and play here."

Joseph said, "These things happen because they are destined to happen. We are not lucky to have the child. But, he will always occupy a special place in our hearts."

I was sitting there with a frozen heart. I was speechless. I was dumb. My eyes were seeing the sky. What was I thinking? Why did not Christopher shout for help? Or did he shout for help and I not did hear?

Allan scolded me.

"How can you be so irresponsible? How could you leave a five-year-old child to play in the beach and kept thinking of some stupid thing?"

"You can give any punishment. I will take it. It is purely my fault. I am not a good mother. It is not your family curse that killed Christopher. It is my negligence." I sobbed uncontrollably. Allan's helpless angry remarks exploded inside my frozen heart with tears flowing down my eyes.

Allan tried to comfort me. He said, "I as a father did not get a single moment to play with him". He took my head and brought it close to his chest.

"I am sorry. I can understand your grief. Instead of sharing the grief with you, I tried to find fault in you.'

Five years rolled by. There has not been a single day without remembering Christopher. I have kept all his toys, the small bat with which he used to hit the ball. When I see his indistinct crayon drawings on the wall, I imagine Christopher coming and forcing me to listen to a story.

Time and tide wait for none.

Chapter 3

* * *

Alok was fast asleep. The whole night, Krishna was suffering from pain. He had to be taken to the wash room three or four times.. The first time he tried to get up from the bed, he fell down. Alok quickly reached him and helped him to get up.

"Do call me whenever you want something or when you want water. Don't try to do anything on your own. My father had fallen once like this and fractured his hand. Don't ever try anything like this". Alok warned his father-in-law.

"Thank you Alok. I have been a nuisance"

"Please don't ever feel like that. You are something very lovable and precious to all of us".

The mobile phone was ringing. Alok was brushing his teeth early in the morning. He quickly rinsed his mouth, washed his face and reached his phone.

"Hi. Alok. Good morning. This is Dr. Kalyani. Could you please come over here any time today when you are free? I want a favour from you".

"Certainly. May be evening. Around 4 pm .".

"That should be alright".

Alok had a shower. He liked to shower in cold water.

The Udupi weather was ideal to have frequent cold water showers.

Revathi came at about 9 am. Alok told her, "Daddy had frequent bathroom visits last night. He drank a lot of water. He was moaning with pain. Why don't we call Dr. Kalyani".

"Is it so? These are common problems when the sugar level goes up. I will check his blood sugar".

She took blood glucose monitoring system. She pricked a sharp needle for a virtually painless pain into the tip of the fore finger of his left hand and applied a tiny drop of blood on the orange test strip pad. The monitor showed a reading of 308.

"Oh! This is hyperglycemia. I will call Dr. Kalyani and ask her to fix a proper dosage. Anyway, I am meeting her after my duty hours".

"Why can't you meet her in the hospital right now Revathi?"

"Oh! I forgot to inform you Alok. She will not be here for another four months. She is visiting her son in the U.S. She is leaving for Bangalore tonight."

"She asked me to meet her. I had scheduled a meeting this evening with her."

"It is better we go and meet her in the house. I will call her up".

Dr Kalyani asked them to come immediately.

"You can take the car Alok."

"Alright daddy".

They drove in the car. Dr. Kalyani's house was a few kilometers away.

"Please do come in". The lady with a broad smile and grace welcomed them.

Alok and Revathi sat opposite each other in the drawing room.

"I will get you some fruit juice."

"Madam I will bring it." Revathi went inside.

"Daddy was suffering from pain last night. He had frequent urination and unusual thirst. I thought it is better you come and visit him".

"Don't worry Alok. These are common in diabetic patients. I have asked Dr. Sudhir Pai to visit him. He will attend and take care of Krishna during my absence. Tonight, I am leaving for Bangalore by flight. I am leaving for New York tomorrow."

Revathi brought the fruit juice glasses. They all had the drink together and seemed to enjoy every drop of it. Revathi collected all the glasses and took them in a tray.

" Revathi. You also come here. I want to talk to you both."

Revathi joined them.

"Alok I need a favour from you. I had to actually give a talk on: 'The emerging role of a modern woman' in the Teresian college in Mysore this Saturday. In fact I am an old student of that college. The programme is scheduled for this Saturday evening at 6 pm. I had given my consent to the college authorities. But my son was unaware of the programme and has sent my flight tickets. So I want you to substitute me and give this talk. Revathi will be there to give you company. She also needs a change of place."

"But then who will take care of Vasundhara's parents?"

"I spoke to Krishna first. He told me that Vasundhara is going to be here on Friday itself. So that should not be a problem."

"Madam what do you want me to do there?"

"Just go there. Listen to his speech. You will have a change of place."

Alok seemed to support Dr. Kalyani's view.

"I agree with you Madam. I enjoy the college life. Young girls blissfully ignorant about the future, enjoying the present, forgetting the past. That is heaven.

Yes Revathi, you should listen to me.

Madam I have a suggestion. We can request the college authorities to let Revathi sing a beautiful song of her choice."

"That is a great idea. I will call up the principal right now."

Dr. Kalyani took up her cell phone. She was about to dial a number.

"Revathi. You like the idea."

"Madam you think I can sing on a platform?"

"Revathi. You have a melodious voice. You prepare well and go. You will sing the song for me."

Dr. Kalyani dialed a number and spoke to the principal. The principal replied that it would be nice to hear how the modern man thinks about the emerging role of a modern woman. She said that she was even happier to hear a choir girl singing a classical musical raag.

Alok and Revathi wished Dr. Kalyani a bon-voyage and left for home.

Alok was driving. Revathi looked apprehensive and remained silent.

"Revathi, what are you thinking about?"

"I don't know what to sing. I just have three days to prepare."

"You don't worry. I will think about this. We will meet at the beach and spend some time in the cool breeze and discuss. You go to the hospital, finish your duty and come directly to the beach."

"Okay. That is fine. I will call you in the evening."

Alok came home and briefed his father-in-law and mother-in-law about the happenings in Dr. Kalyani's house."

Vasundhara's mother, Janaki was a bit unhappy about this Mysore trip.

"Only you two are going?"

Krishna replied: "Don't talk stupid. They are grown up adults, who are well aware of their responsibilities. This is the twenty first century. You should learn to move on with the changing times."

"I am sorry. I did not mean anything to hurt Alok's feelings."

"No Mom. I know you. I care as much for your daughter as you do, if not more. I will speak to Vasundhara also. If she does not like this, I don't mind dropping this program."

"Oh! Then I will be branded as an idiot and an old fashioned lady."

Krishna replied, "At last good sense has prevailed on you. You talk to Vasundhara. I am sure she will be very happy. She is coming here on Friday."

Alok was just writing notes for his lecture. He immediately thought of Revathi. That beautiful face was like the full moon. She had that charm, sweet voice. She could present herself in a very graceful manner. Why not I make her sing that alaap which captured me even before I saw her. She said that it is raag Malkauns. We will follow it up with a beautiful Hindola song. Could it be a devotional one? No, that may not suit a college function. The talk should glorify the woman. A song that suits would be the Hindola composition from the film Naandi. The song glorifies the woman as the real source of energy and inspiration for the entire human race. The woman in the role of a mother, as a wife, asa sister as a daughter. The modern woman has to perform all these roles and work outside as well. I think my talk will focus on these and Revathi will do the singing part. I am sure she will win the hearts. Let her steal the show. Let that become her moment of glory.

The phone bell rang.

"Hi! It is me Vasundhara. I hope you have not forgotten me in writing your magnum opus. It is great that a scholar like Dr. Kalyani has picked you for giving a talk in such a prestigious college. I am very proud of you. Go ahead. I am confident that you will do a great job. I spoke to Uma, my classmate, a professor in that college. She teaches physics. She told that she will shoot your entire programme in her video camera and send it to me. I am just very excited"

"I think you have already put it up in your Whatsapp group".

"Sure. Any objection?"

"Certainly not. My fear is that if it turns out to be a fiasco."

"It certainly will not"

"Thanks for your encouragement. Revathi is also accompanying me."

"Nice. But why?"

"Dr. Kalyani felt that Revathi will have a change of place."

"I know, I really pity that girl. Her husband thinks his only duty is to pay all the monthly bills. He never stays at home. Sometimes he is away from her for two to three months. After her child's death she had been driven to depression. She committed suicide attempts twice. On both the occasions Dr. Kalyani saved her. She has been a great source of strength to her. Since she asked you to do this, it is good you accepted it."

"Revathi is going to sing in that function."

"I am very happy to know you are also contributing something to make her happy."

"Bye then. I will meet you on the night of Friday."

"I would have left for Mysore in the evening."

"Okay it is alright. Wish you all the success."

"Thank you".

Alok was thinking about his mother. What a strong woman she was. He kept thinking about her. His father was an idealist. He believed that society came first and then the home. He taught him the importance of human values of peace, tolerance, respecting the opponent. He didn't believe in defeating a person. He wanted to win as a person. His mother didn't believe in dreaming and had virtually no time to listen to him. She believed in the ground reality of a situation and faced it with pragmatism and patience.

When he told his mother about Vasundhara, she was a bit apprehensive. She asked him, "Why should an aristocratic girl like her ever think of marrying a college teacher like you?"

He said, "She is a science student. No one pays attention in Language classes. But she loves my classes. She is very much influenced by my lectures. She likes poetry the best. She comes and sits in M.A English classes. She seems to be mature."

"But you don't seem to be immature in front of her. I only hope it is not just infatuation".

"No Mom, it appears to be true love".

Finally, mother gave consent for our marriage. Vasundhara's parents had planned for a very grand marriage. But, he opted for a very simple marriage. He told them very clearly that at most he would become the principal of the college. He could not afford a very luxurious life. But, he promised a happy life and raise a decent family.

Krishna, his father-in -law was very much impressed with his views. His mother-in-law was not very happy with his house in Bangalore. She first thought of relocating him to Udupi. She told him that he could start a college of his own in Bantwal, where she had a huge ancestral property. He was not enthusiastic about this proposal.

Finally, Vasundhara's parents let them live the way they wanted to live.

Vasundhara was dedicated to her job as a wife. She liked his mother's skills in her multifarious activities. She liked his father's views. But, she was more supportive to his mother's view that family should have a greater priority over social service.

These two women gave him the best moments in his life. His children, Adithya and Apoorva, have given him the most beautiful moments in his life.

He wanted to have a daughter. He wanted to love his daughter the way Vasundhara's parents loved her. A daughter is like the raag Hindola. She sings the most melodious tunes bringing waves of the highest state of bliss. When she leaves for her husband's home, she brings the sweetest songs with the saddest thoughts of memory. When she comes back home, she brings a wave of happiness. She makes everyone's moods swing in between the extremities of happiness and sadness. He wished he had a daughter of his own. When the doctor told him that Vasundhara cannot have a third child, he was in for a big disappointment. But it is the will of God.

He had almost completed his notes. He had planned the programme. Revathi will sing Malkauns alaap and follow it up by the Hindola composition from the film "Chandramukhi, Praanasakhi".

Chapter Four

* * *

ALOK:

Revathi had called me up. She appeared to be more enthusiastic. I walked towards the beach. She was approaching me from a distance. She was dressed up in a very nice blue skirt. Her long beautiful arms looked as if they welcomed me for a warm embrace. We sat on the sands of the beach. It was a very pleasant evening. The cool breeze was moving through our bodies.

I said, "As you were walking, I was reminded of a beautiful romantic poem by Byron. I will recite this poem for you."

"Okay Sir, I am really in a romantic mood today. Go on."

Alok started to recite the poem.

She walks in beauty, like the night
Of cloudless climes and starry skies;
And all that's best of dark and bright
Meet in her aspect and her eyes;
Thus mellowed to that tender light
Which heaven to gaudy day denies.

One shade the more, one ray the less,
Had half impaired the nameless grace
Which waves in every raven tress,
Or softly lightens o'er her face;
Where thoughts serenely sweet express,
How pure, how dear their dwelling-place.

And on that cheek, and o'er that brow,
So soft, so calm, yet eloquent,
The smiles that win, the tints that glow,
But tell of days in goodness spent,
A mind at peace with all below,
A heart whose love is innocent!

"What a lovely poem!"

"Actually this poem was written by Byron in response to seeing his cousin, Lady Wilmot Horton, in a mourning dress at a party. This poem is an analysis of the many facets that come together to form a beautiful woman. The poem reveals a woman's beauty by descriptions of her physical, spiritual and intellectual traits."

"No wonder. I can understand why Vasundhara fell in love with you."

"Umm?"

"Your voice is romantic, resonant. When you were reading those lines, it seemed like music. It is love."

I told Revathi that she would be singing the Malkauns alaap first and follow it up by the Hindola composition "Chandramukhi, Praanasakhi".

"Are you making it a musical event? You are supposed to talk about the emerging role of the modern woman."

"I know. But a lecture about human values becomes more attractive when it is interleaved with a melodious voice.

That is the reason I have chosen this song which makes a woman an angel condescending from the heavens to protect the human race."

"Thank you Professor Alok. Your resonant voice appears to emerge from the sky and for a moment fills the soul of the listener."

"Thanks for the compliment".

"So, what is our programme on Saturday?"

"We are leaving on Friday at 4 pm. We will travel by train. We will reach Mysore early in the morning. Vasundhara's friend Uma called me up and invited us to stay at her house. We will freshen up and have breakfast there. We will visit Srirangapatna, which is a beautiful place. We will visit the Kaveri river at Sangam. We will sit in the shade under the trees for some time. We will talk for a while. We can have lunch in a good hotel. We can come back at about 4 pm to Uma's house. We will refresh ourselves and get dressed up. The college will send a cab to pick us up and we will return by train the same night.""I should now start practicing that alaap. Can I get that song in Youtube?" Revathi asked.

"I don't know. But I have a collection of Hindola songs recorded in this pen drive. Have you heard that song ever?" I asked her.

"No, I don't remember. But I think my music teacher had taught me that song. I think I should practice that."

She took that pen drive. She bolted herself in her room. Luck was on her side that day; she was all alone in the house. Gracey had gone to Mangalore along with her sons for some marriage function.

She played the alaap over and over. She found out the song "Chandramukhi, Pranasakhi". I had explained the meaning of the song pretty well. The song is sung on the occasion of a pregnant woman wearing green bangles. The colour green symbolizes prosperity and happiness. It is like the spring season where nature is in its most beautiful form.

She had found her voice. Through the alaap she was pouring her feelings out. Then the song started. She was enjoying the song more and more. For once, she felt that she should become pregnant and experience all the joy and pain once again.

Back at work, she was cheerful, enthusiastic. Her close friend Sr. Juliana told her,

"You are looking more beautiful these days with your face radiating with happiness. I would love to see you always like this. What is the matter?"

"Julie, I am going to sing at a college function. I am practicing a lot. It is giving me a lot of joy."

"Very nice. Music has really that divine power... Your phone is ringing."

"Thank you Julie. It is him. I will just go out for a few minutes. Please manage."

"Hi! Alok."

"We will meet at the beach. Come a little earlier. We will spend a little longer time".

"Sure."

They were seated on the sands of the beach. She had come dressed in a skirt. She was looking like a young college girl. I was in an informal attire i.e jeans and tee shirt. We were looking at the sea. She told me,

"Hold my hand. We will walk together."

"How come you are so condescending on this poor lover?

Sorry, I shouldn't have used the word lover... Friend?"

"Now you can take the liberty of calling me a lover. You know why? I am very happy. I am excited. I found my rhythm, my alaap was perfect. There came out a voice which was a sweet melody to my own ears. Alok, I am going to sing very nicely."

"So, that is great news. I have finalized the text of my speech."

"Alok, have you booked the return ticket?"

"No, not yet. We will spend some more time in Mysore. We will talk a lot. We will visit some places".

"You have spoken my mind". She held my hands firmly.

"Have you informed Allan about this?"

"He asked me to go and agreed that I do require a change."

"Where is he right now?"

"He is in Goa. He is having good business there. I came to know that he is in a live-in relation with his girl friend. He likes to stay most of the time in Goa. He hardly comes to Udupi. Even if he does, he just meets me in the hospital and goes away. But he is very much concerned about his mother and his brothers."

We left that place bidding good bye to each other and planned to meet the next day.

The next day, Friday morning, we had arrived at the Mysore City Railway Station.

It was Uma. She had come in her car to the railway station.

"Alok, I am in the car parking area. My car is a Toyota Etios. Note down the number. Come down straight here."

"Thank you. Yes. I have spotted your car."

We moved to the car parking area.

"Hey. I am Uma", Uma greeted Revathi and me. The driver helped us to take our suit cases and put it into the car.

We reached a newly constructed house. Uma told us that they had demolished the old house and constructed a new one. The house was very modern. The TV screen was so big that one felt as if he was sitting in a theatre. The huge leather sofas, the carpets, the dining table, everything reflected the sophisticated style of living of Uma.

She was speaking of her college days and friendship with Vasundhara. We were seated around a small round table for breakfast. We were having breakfast. She said to her domestic help, "After they go, you lock up the house. Prepare some good food. Prepare paayasa. I will come in the afternoon."

She said, "I was actually in the U.S at the time of your marriage. So I could not attend your marriage. Vasundhara had sent some photos. I remember how Vasundhara missed all her other classes to attend your English poetry classes."

I replied, "Vasundhara had told me about your stylish accent. She told me that you are a fabulous tennis player. You represented the college in some tournaments."

"Gone are those days. My husband is busy with his company. We have a software company. We have about one hundred employees. I don't want to leave this job. We have made it a point to meet on weekends. Our meeting place could be Mysore or Bangalore."

Revathi wanted to go out and be free, to talk freely and spend time with me. Uma turned to Revathi and started talking to her.

"So, that is the singing nightingale from Udupi. Vasundhara told me that you have a beautiful voice. My voice is very rough. I went to piano classes in my school days. But, I was more interested in sports. That was the end of my musical career. But I love listening to classical western symphonies. I love Hindustani music.

"You can just move around Mysore and come back for lunch, rest for a while. During the evenings, we are in the college. You can take my car".

"Thank you. We have actually booked a cab. Vasundhara had told me that you are a great host."

"I have to conduct a university practical examination here in a college. So I am going out. We will meet at lunch.

Thank you… Bye then. ”

Without waiting for any reply, she drove off in a car.”

“My God, she is so dynamic. That is the modern woman. Where are her children? ”

“She has two girls. Both the girls are in a boarding school in Ooty”.

“Oh! My God. I think that is the real modern woman.”

We set out for Srirangapatna. We straight went to the temple. I was explaining to Revathi, “Srirangapatna is replete with history. Tippu Sultan had made this as his capital. He used to pray to the God every day from his palace. From a corner of his palace he could see the topmost point of the Gopura. Gopura is a tall tower like structure that you see in the front portion of the temple.” We saw the GolGumbaz. Revathi was behaving just like a school girl.

She said, “Today my desire to live again has generated. I don’t want to die. I would like to sing on the river side. I want to run aimlessly in these green paddy and sugarcane fields.”

We visited the temple. I was observing her curiously as she took the mangalarathi and the theertha. She started singing some devotional songs and went three times in the corridor round the sanctum sanctorum. I blindly followed her. I was observing each and every step of hers. I could not stop observing her.

When we came out of the temple and entered the cab, I asked her, “Do you visit temples? You seem to be used to all these procedures. You took the mangalaarathi, the theertha …”

“Yeah. I am. I visit the Udupi Krishna temple practically every Saturday evening. It gives me an aesthetic emotional pleasure. It is divine.”

“We will visit a church here in Ganjam. I had visited this church in one of my school excursions”.

She straight went inside the church. She met a priest

and introduced herself that she was an inmate of the convent in Udupi and gave the reference of Fr. Bernard Desouza.

The priest was very polite and asked us to have a cup of tea. He explained us the history of the church.

We had now come to the banks of the Kaveri. We sat there for some time looking at the beauty of the flowing river. Revathi took every opportunity to hold Alok's hands and put her arm round his neck. She seemed to be enjoying every moment of the day.

We were back for lunch. The food was very tasty. Uma had brought some sweets.

I was enjoying the food and sweets and everything around was absolutely perfect.

"Revathi, taste this sweet."

When Uma offered to serve sweets, Revathi said, "No please. That affects my throat".

"I have to go to the college. I have some work. At about 5.30 pm. the college will send the car. Please rest for a while."

After Uma had gone, we were seated in the drawing room. I was reading the news paper.

"Revathi, why did you refuse the sweets?"

"After my son's death I have stopped eating sweets."

"Sorry. I was not aware of that."

We entered the portals of the college in the evening. Uma was waiting for us. She led us to the principal's chambers.

"Please be seated Professor. Dr. Kalyani is an old student of our college. She is a passionate singer. She used to sing in all our functions. Even after she became a doctor she used to give concerts. She has studied a lot of books on musicology. She is an eminent critic and writes regularly in some papers. She recommended your name and you have been kind enough to accept our invitation".

Looking at Revathi, she said, "I was told that you have a beautiful voice. We are very happy to have you here.

Please have your tea."

The function started. Alok was seated in the dais along with the principal and mother superior. The girls stood up for the college prayer. Revathi was seated in the front row. I was observing Revathi. She was singing loudly. It appeared as if she knew the whole prayer.

The college principal, in her welcome speech, said the function was a part of the international year of women. She said, "It is very nice to have a gentleman, a Professor to talk about the role of the working women. Girls, you will be interested to know that he is a great teacher of poetry. Sir, I was told that some of the girls used to leave their science classes to attend your poetry and drama classes. It is indeed very nice of you to have accepted our invitation. On behalf of the college and management I extend you a very warm welcome. Over to Prof. Alok Vyasa Thirtha."

I stood up. Revathi was observing me in awe. I thought that I looked very decent and tall. She had never seen me in this formal attire. I was dressed in a dark black suit with a beautiful tie. I started my speech, "I have an interesting thing to tell you. It is true that many students used to leave their classes and attend my class. That is the power of poetry. And one more thing, one such student eventually became my life partner. She wanted to be here, but could not do so, because she has to take care of her parents. That is the woman I am talking to you about this evening. But she doesn't want to miss anything. She has asked her classmate Prof Uma, your Physics professor, to shoot the entire function and send it to her.

Women are God's greatest gift to mankind. Today when you go to an interview for a job, they look out for a person who can perform multifunctional activities. He or she should have computer knowledge. The candidate should have had some extracurricular activity. The candidate should be a debater, a sports person. He or she should participate in all the activities of the company ..etc. He or she should be eclectic. But, please remember, dear students, your mother has been performing all these activities since time immemorial.

The child grows in the womb of a woman for nine months and emerges into this earth and sees the light of the world. Whether the child is inside her or outside her, the mother goes on protecting the child. The role played by the mother will remain in any person's memory for a very long time throughout the journey of his life. When she is alive, she is there with us making us eat, speak and walk. The first syllable that a child utters is a letter from the word mother. It could me amma or maa or whatever. Then she teaches you to express your feelings through words. I remember my mother holding my hands and make me write the Kannada alphabets. The names of the seasons, the Gods, the Goddesses, the stories, the characters in our epics, I remember them even today. That is because my mother recited those verses and explained the story behind it. One such incident is vivid in my memory even today. It is the situation in which Kunti approaches Karna for a favour.

In the Mahabharata, Karna was born to the unwed mother Kunthi. A great war was supposed to happen between Arjuna and Karna. Kunthi couldn't lose either of them as both of them were her sons. She approached Karna for a favour. The story goes on and Karna promised her "ninnaya veeraraivaranu noyisenu, rajeeva sakhanaane.

'I will not hurt your five brave sons. This is my promise. I swear it on the name of Rajeeva sakha'. Rajeeva sakha, the Sun. The Sun is the friend of the lotus flower."

Some of these words and lines were taught by my mother. This could be the story of any one.

In my youth, she was looking for a girl who I could spend my life with".

I paused for a while and continued with a softer tone.

"In my case, the girl came from my class room."

The entire audience clapped and seemed to be enjoying the lecture.

"Those days, we believed in the wisdom of our parents. When a woman enters into a man's life, life appears beautiful, more colourful. You are in the seventh heaven.

Back at work, we realize that we have to raise a family of our own. We dream of building a small house in the distant woods and hills near a river. We want to listen to the soft humming of birds. But, that cannot happen. We also hear the raven. We have to work for a living. Dreams are beautiful. But to achieve and realize them, we have to work. We descend to the earth from the heavens. When we start facing the realities, another phase of life begins. It is the woman again in the form of man's wife, who cheers the man up and asks him not to lose hope. She is the real source of inspiration. She is the strength, the source of energy that drives you to work.

In many respects, from the late-nineteenth-century, celebration of the New Woman represented a turn away from the cult of a true womanhood. Higher education, professional employment, political involvement, and athletics were among the areas into which women now demanded entrance. Instead of selflessness, they pursued self-development, individuality, and independence.

Unsurprisingly, many Americans greeted this new style of femininity with anxiety and disapproval, predicting a general disintegration of home life and national prosperity. However, as a black club woman, Dora Cole argued, the New Woman was really just like the old one – but with an added element of 'joyous expansion':

'It has become a necessity for her to find an outlet for all this energy, hence her interest in church and state, in all that is on the earth or in the waters under the earth.

Look when they are at home, is she not a more intelligent companion, a wiser, more judicious mother, a more stimulating and sympathetic friend?'

This was an excerpt I borrowed from the writing about a woman. I think the situation has not changed much since then.

The working woman is stronger, physically and mentally. In the new role, she emerges even more powerful. In spite of her busy schedule of work, she is available to every member in the family. She is a lone fighter with the entire family behind her. But, what about her family members? They can only shed a tear of appreciation or sympathy as a gift. What we have to give her is pure love.

I thought that we could conclude this programme with a beautiful song from an old Kannada film. This song is becoming more and more beautiful when I hear it over and over. There are two factors about this song. This is set to the raag Hindola.

Hindola is a very beautiful raaga on the pentatonic scale. It does not make use of the rishabha and the panchama. It is a very soothing sweet raaga used generally to carry the feelings of melancholy, devotion and submission. When sung, it produces a feeling of pathos, sweetness, a feeling that keeps you haunting. It is mesmerizing. It is hypnotic.

The word Hindola means a swing. Oscillations in classical physics represent a periodic motion between two extreme ends. When the pendulum swings to one extreme end there is a restoring force pulling it back. The same thing happens when it goes to the other extreme. Our emotions, feelings and thoughts are just like the Hindola. In this particular song, the poet uses the feeling of the green bangles, which a pregnant woman is made to wear. It is an occasion of ecstasy. It is like the earth decorated with greenery in the spring. The leaves dancing in bright colours, the wind blowing through them, humming sometimes, roaring sometimes with the onset of monsoon. The earth seems to be complacent, with the birds chirping, the peacocks singing and happiness permeating. This symbolizes a pregnant woman. Perhaps, this is the happiest and the most painful moment in a woman's life.

The poet uses the Hindola raag to such perfection that we feel that we are lost in the song. My friend Revathi will sing this raaga for you. The song is about the different phases of a woman's life, a woman as a mother, as a wife. The poet finally goes on to say that, she, the woman is the source of real energy of mankind and it is she that makes the life cycle eternal and in a continuum. The poet is telling the woman all these facts which she is blissfully unaware of.

I came across a similar poem in English which conveys a similar meaning. I will read out these lines for you.

She walketh veiled and sleeping
For she knoweth not her power;
She obeyeth but the pleading
Of her heart, and the high leading
Of her soul unto this hour
Slow advancing, halting and creeping'
Comes the woman to the hour!
She walketh veiled and sleeping
For she knoweth not her power;

Yes. The woman is not aware of her tremendous potential. Shakespeare said:

"Frailty thy name is woman". Woman was considered to have a wavering mind. But, I always look at a woman as a rock, who can take all the forces that hit her. She allows all the waves of the sea to come and bounce back.

In our mythology, the woman is depicted as the cause of all wars and destruction.

I beg to differ from some great poets. I would prefer to say,

'*Woman thou art divinity*'.

Thank you."

There was a thunderous applause from the girls. Many stood up and cheered.

Revathi sat on the dias. She was draped in a beautiful light cream coloured saree. Dr. Kalyani had advised her not go in a skirt or a gown. She was looking gorgeous and graceful.

The students and professors were looking at her. They seemed very happy by her presence.

"She is awesome." They said to themselves.

She sang a two line stotra invoking the presence of Vinayaka. She started the Malkauns alaap. As the melodious musical waves of the alaap started, her emotions seemed to melt. It was a very melodious rendition with the musical notes touching the crescendo. The soft timbre, pristine and clear musical notes were in perfect rhythmic flow. It was like the Ganga river in its purest form near its origins, flowing gently by the side of the snowy mountains slowly, majestically and yet streaming energetically. A piano player who had come to support the college orchestra simply closed his eye and spontaneously played very softly, supporting the alaap.

The audience was just held in a trance. The students, the teachers were holding their eyes fixed at Revathi's beauty. Some of them wanted to concentrate on her voice alone and had closed their eyes.

Every one clapped after the alaap was over. Revathi folded her hands and gestured thankfully. By this time a girl, who was very proficient in playing veena came and joined Revathi on the stage unsolicited. She asked Revathi nonverbally, "Can I accompany you?". Revathi nodded approvingly with a broad smile. The orchestra group had a music arranger and a conductor. They seemed to be very enthusiastic. He approached Revathi and said, "You sing that alaap once again for us. In between the stanzas we will run the veena bit again and we will play a bit on the flute as a prelude just after your alaap and all the violinists will accompany you in perfect rhythm very softly. Please do this favour?"

She started the alaap once again. This time she sang even more melodiously. The piano tones playing softly decorated her voice. She started the Hindola composition. Since I had explained the meaning of the song, everyone seemed to enjoy her song.

After the song was over, the entire audience stood up for a standing ovation.

Revathi thanked the musicians.

Revathi stood on the stage together and bowed to the audience.

Uma was waiting for us outside.

"We need to rush. It is nearing 8.30 pm. You have to catch your train. Come on," she said. She drove us to her house. As she was driving, she said, "It was a beautiful speech Alok. You have a low baritone in your voice. No wonder Vasundhara fell for you. And you Revathi, you are an angel. You have everything a woman should have.

The alaap, the song, everything was simply beautiful."

"When the musicians started accompanying me, I was a bit apprehensive. Luckily, I found my rhythm correctly".

"You are truly blessed."

"I should thank Alok and Dr. Kalyani,"Revathi replied.

They packed their suitcases and called a cab. They thanked Uma. As they were travelling in the cab, the driver asked

"Where to?"

Alok said "Railway station"

Trains to Udupi were cancelled due to heavy rains in the ghat-section. The notice board displayed at the railway station entrance dampened their spirits.

"Oh! My God. Come on. Then there must be no buses

as well. Shall we go back to Uma's house?"Alok asked Revathi.

"No please. Not now."

"Then we will go to the convent next to the college. You stay there tonight. I will stay in this platform.

"No. I don't want to stay in the convent. I will also sit with you in this platform. See there. There are so many waiting like us. Or , shall we go to a decent hotel and stay for the night?"

"But I don't have so much money in my wallet. I don't have sufficient balance in the card either."

"Never mind. I have my credit card. Come on."

We went to a good hotel near the railway station. There was only one room available. The hotel manager said, "We can provide an additional mattress. You have to pay for that."

"Okay. That is fine."

"Rs 1,200 Sir."

Revathi took her card and swiped it.

They came into the room.

"At last.."

"Alok I have to change my dress. But I don't have a night dress. What do I do?"

"Come. You buy a new night dress. There seem to be lots of shops in the surroundings."

"I don't mind sleeping in this saree. But it is a beautiful saree and it is not mine".

"Then…?"

"Kalyani madam asked me to wear this. She didn't want me to go in skirts and other dresses which I usually wear".

We went down. We found a good shop to buy a night dress for her.

We were very tired from the happenings of the day. But nevertheless, we seemed to enjoy the flush of freedom.

After reaching the room, there was a little debate about who would take the cot and who would sleep on the mattress.

After some debate it was decided that they would put both the beds on the ground. They pushed the cot to the wall. They slept.

Revathi went inside the bath room and entered in the transparent night dress revealing the cream coloured bra and her beautiful body. She appeared sexy.

"How do you think was the day?" I asked her.

"It was beautiful. I am enjoying every moment. You didn't say anything about my dress."

"It is very beautiful. You look very sexy. I only pray to God that I do not do anything immoral".

"Come on Alok. I want you to enjoy my body. I am very glad that all this happened. I am all yours." She spoke in a low husky voice.

She put her long arm round my neck and passionately kissed my lips.

I asked her after a pause, "Are we committing a sin?"

"Certainly not. I love you Alok. I want a child. Please don't disappoint me".

We embraced and hugged each other for a long time. Finally we were united in body and soul.

I could not sleep. Revathi slept peacefully. Her beautiful face was glowing with happiness. 'Where are we going? Have I been immoral? Is this not infidelity?' I repeatedly played these questions in my mind.

Revathi turned aside and looked at me.

"Why don't you sleep?" She again came close to me and went on kissing me passionately.

I looked at her and said, "You are beautiful. Your beautiful body, those supple breasts are tempting me".

"The best thing to overcome a temptation is to yield it. I am enjoying. You must forget everything and enjoy these supple breasts. I am all yours. I want a child… I want a child."

She was crying in an emotional burst, letting out all hear latent sadness. I embraced her and kissed her. She reciprocated my gestures very lovingly.

That morning, I got up to my mobile ringtone.

"Where are you Alok? Last night it was raining heavily. Phones were dead. There was no response from your phone," Vasundhara was speaking anxiously.

"Thanks for calling. Actually, I thought of coming back to Udupi to join you. All the trains and buses moving towards Udupi were cancelled. I could get a bus to Bangalore. I am here in our home in Bangalore. My publisher's agent is coming from London. He said they want to review the progress of my book. I have to take a conference call with him. I have to attend the video conference with the editorial team," I lied.

"Where is Revathi staying?"

I was shocked. I purposely did not utter Revathi's name in an attempt to hide the last night's incidents.

"I left her at her friend's house somewhere near Koramangala. She said she would catch a bus to Udupi the next morning.

I was lying to her very easily.

Revathi laughingly said, "You liar!"

"I have spoken a little bit of truth also. The only lie is that we didn't leave for Bangalore last night. I am leaving for Bangalore this morning and you are going to Udupi. I forgot to tell you about my video conference with the editorial team and the publisher's Bangalore agent."

"Okay. We part here.. to meet again at Udupi". There was a sense of sadness in her tone.

"Don't worry. We will create another occasion to meet like this".

"Just the two of us.."

"Certainly". I promised.

Chapter Five

* * *

Revathi:

I was dressing up in my hospital uniform. I thought of meeting Krishna and enquire about his health. I thought it would be very difficult to face Vasundhara. I reminded myself, "Let me maintain the same story line authored by Alok. He will not be there, any way".

I resumed my normal life in Udupi. It was almost three weeks after I had the unprotected sex with Alok. Being a nurse, I was aware of the fact that I should take a pregnancy test at home. I took the test at home and confirmed that I was pregnant. I was excited. I thought of informing Alok. But I should inform Gracey. But what do I tell her? She knows that Allan is not sleeping with me. He visits me in the hospital only once. I have not had sex with him ever since my son passed away. Should I come out of this family? Should I have an abortion?

"No. I can never do that. I should protect my child," I said to myself.

She seemed to have made up her mind. Her pregnancy seemed to have increased her will power.

"I have to tell Allan about this," she said to herself.

The cell phone was ringing.

"Hey. It is me Alok. I am sending a link. Open that and see your beautiful face. Listen to your melodious song. It has been put up on YouTube. Uma sent me this link. It has come out beautifully. A student had covered the entire function very professionally. She got it edited and put it up on YouTube. There are already more than thirty thousand likes and excellent comments. Dr. Kalyani has also commented. She has written, "I saw the Goddess Saraswathi in Revathi. It is divine.

Another good news. My book has been accepted for publication."

"That is great news. Thank you Alok, for this trip. I want to talk to you about something very personal. I will come down to Bangalore. We have to meet."

"How is it possible?" Vasundhara is here.

"I am pregnant with your child, Alok."

"That is great."

"But how do we disclose this?"

"Oh! I didn't think of this at all. Alright we will again meet. But not in Bangalore, maybe in Mysore. Don't worry. We will face the consequences. We will sail or sink together. Take care. I am with you."

I thought of committing suicide. But that would be a murder of my child. Allan is not bothered. But I have to tell Gracey. She knows that I am not sleeping with Allan. If she asks me who?...

What should I answer.?

As she walked towards her bedroom, she saw the pregnancy test kit lying on the table. The room was messy. She planned to put things in order to restore normalcy. She was feeling lazy, tired and restless.

When she opened her small suit case, she discovered a few sheets of paper. They were some abstract drawings made using crayons by Christopher. She observed each drawing. Her face was lit with happiness. Tears melted and started pouring. Christopher seemed to be telling a story holding the sheet of the crumpled paper.

"Where are you my child?" She kept sobbing.

She was thinking of the previous year.

The Previous year:

Revathi:

I was in a deep pensive mood. I thought of going to Goa to spend a few days with Allan. I thought of joining Allan to start a new life after Christopher's death.

When I had called him, he had said "I am in Mangalore right now. I am in my village. Come down if you wish to".

I went to Mangalore. Allan has an estate and a small house near Panambur. Most of the time he travels in the cab. He said, "I will be able to clear my loan in another three years. When the business is really good, I get a lot of money. Otherwise I prefer to stay here. I love this place. Once the loan is cleared, we will make our family here. But you cannot have a child from me. I have vowed not to have sex anymore. We will adopt a child."

"But why? Allan what happened?"

Allan:

My son Christopher was dead. In one of my visits to our church, I met Father Bernard. He was very sad to know of Christopher's death.

He said, "It is a curse on our family. If the first child dies, then you will have no more children. I don't know whether to believe this or not. But it did happen in the case of your uncle. He lost his wife after he lost his first child. His wife committed suicide and he eventually joined our church."

"You mean to say, all this had already happened to

Dominic uncle?"

"Surely. Go and talk to him. He has lots of things to tell you".

I went to Mangalore. Dominic uncle was almost eighty. But he was alert. He could talk clearly. He was weak, but he could manage to carry out his normal activities.

"Come on dear son. You look just like your father."

"Uncle, Fr. Bernard asked me to meet you."

Uncle Dominic replied, "We have decided to transfer our property in your name. In this village we have about forty acres of agricultural land. There is a small farm house in Goa."

"Who is looking after that property?"

"I myself go there once a month or once in two months. Your brother George comes once in two months or three months."

"Does George come to Goa?"

"Yes. He helps us in some of our works. In spite of his waywardness, he has a kind heart.

Now you should take care of Gracey, and your brothers. Your main task would be to make your irresponsible brothers realize and make them responsible human beings. They too are your family."

"Now what is this curse you and Fr. Bernard were talking about?"

"Didn't Father tell you about this?".

Uncle Bernard began, "My mother used to always tell me this. My uncle had married a beautiful girl. She was a very immature girl. She used to dance, drink and move with all sorts of boys. My uncle discovered that she had a relation with her boyfriend and she continued to have that even after marriage. She was pregnant with his child even before the marriage.

One day, uncle thought of counseling my aunt and stop the relation. He took her to the beach and asked her to terminate the pregnancy and stop the affair. She wanted to continue the affair. She refused to terminate the pregnancy and asked him for a divorce. In a fit of anger he held her hands firmly and dragged her to the beach into the waters almost neck deep and pushed her. The strong waves of the sea carried the pregnant woman. Her body could not be traced. My brother was arrested. The court tried him and he was found guilty. He was sentenced to life imprisonment. They say that the soul of the pregnant woman is taking revenge on our family. Our fears were not unconfounded; my child died nine days after its birth. My wife who had heard this entire story committed suicide. I joined the church as a manager".

After listening to this sad story, I returned to Udupi. I met Fr. Bernard.

Fr. Bernard returned from his painful memories, "When I got the news of your child's death, I thought of asking you not to have any physical relationship with your wife. The very thought of a lady of our family becoming pregnant scares me. You stay back in your village. Let her live in Udupi. She is any way doing a noble job."

"So, that is it Revathi. I don't want you to become pregnant. I love you so much that I am afraid of losing you. I do not believe in these stupid stories. But how can this happen to us?" I kept on sobbing.

"Whenever I come to Udupi and sit on the sands of the beach, I ask the sea. 'Where did you take Christopher?' I have walked into the sea asking the waves to carry me. Some fear, some thoughts about my family, my mother and you, Revathi makes me take a u-turn and come back. Then I come back, bolt myself inside and weep. I have done this at least ten times in these months. When I go to the church, I try meditating. When they give these sermons on the greatness and kindness of God and his abundant blessings… and such other things, they appear to be meaningless, they appear to be dry words which cannot instill in me any devotion. I do not want to blame or hate God. It is my karma which I have to carry on my shoulders.

So , Revathi we will live like this. You stay back in Udupi. You go back to work. I will take of our property and my uncle. I could not serve my father. I would like to make it up by serving him." I tried explaining Revathi why we could not have a child of our own after Christopher.

Revathi opened the link sent by Alok in her laptop. She thought that she had sung really well.

'He is very handsome'. She said to herself. He is forty-five years old. I am thirty two. Alok looked handsome in his black suit. He is very romantic. His low baritone voice excited her. There were rave reviews. Many girls liked Alok's voice. Many women wrote in awe about his views on women.

The mobile phone rang. She picked up the phone and said, "Hello".

"Am I speaking to Revathi? This is Sandhya Rao from Chennai. I got your number from Teresian College. My dear girl, your voice is divine. After a long time I heard a voice of this kind. The shruti, rhythm and laya are perfect. Your voice is very melodious. My girl, I just want to come there and hug you. I am coming to Bangalore for an audio recording for a Kannada film, may be next week. Please meet me there. In Chennai the famous music director Shankar Vasishta is in search of a voice like this. He wants a singer who can sing Hindola like this. I will introduce you to him. I am sure he will just fall in love with your voice."

"Thank you Madam. Please do call me."

She was excited. She played her song once again on YouTube. She was very happy.

She took her phone and dialed Alok's number.

His phone was switched off. She tried after some time. She didn't want to talk to Vasundhara.

But why was his phone switched off? She managed to find out his college number. When she dialed the number, the office manager told her that Alok was on a long leave and he was admitted to the hospital. She dialed Vasundhara's phone number.

"Hi. This is me Revathi. How are you Vasundhara?"

"I am fine. How are you? I saw your video on YouTube. Your singing was divine"

"Thank you". She anxiously asked. "How is Alok?"

"He fell down in the classroom while lecturing. A colleague brought him home in his car. We immediately admitted him. He is down with hypertension. He was all alone and used to write for hours together."

"Can I come and visit him in the hospital?"

"Sure. Alok will be happy to see you."

"Thank you. Which hospital?"

"St. John's hospital."

She packed a few things. She was feeling anxious. 'Jesus! Pardon me if you think that I have committed a sin'. She prayed for a while.

'Let anything happen to me. I want Alok to be happy and healthy'. She said to herself.

She booked a cab. She locked her house. She was very worried. She forgot all her body pain. She ran to the bus stand and boarded a luxury bus.

While she was travelling in the bus, she tried to sleep, but could hardly sleep. She just wanted to go and talk to him. She said to herself,

'I have to be discreet, poised and control my emotions. I know the cause of his hypertension. He is surely struggling to tell Vasundhara about our relationship."

She had fallen into a slumber. When she woke up, the bus had touched the outskirts of Bangalore. The pre-monsoon showers had set in Bangalore. The first rains had soaked Bangalore. The smell of the earth was a treat to the pregnant lady.

Revathi got down from the bus. She took a cab to St.

John's hospital. She was quite familiar with the huge hospital. She rang up Vasundhara, who gave her the directions. Revathi went straight near the special room. Vasundhara came out and handed over the attendant's pass.

"They are very strict here. Only one attendant is allowed. You just sit near him. He has not been talking for the past few days. Please try to talk to him. He seems to be suffering from a pain deep within himself. He has withdrawn himself into a shell. Your coming here is a blessing for me. You go inside and talk to him. I have not even bathed for two days. I will refresh myself.

I will go home and prepare lunch for both of us. My cousin will stay overnight and you stay with me tonight. I want to talk for a while and de-stress myself."

Revathi nodded approvingly. Vasundhara gave her the attendant's pass.

She went inside his room. In spite of her determination to be restrained, tears flowed from her eyes when she saw Alok lying on the bed speechless. The sparkle in his eyes had gone. The brightness in his face seemed to have faded away. She went close to him. She placed her hand on his forehead. She held his hands and pressed it firmly.

Alok opened his eyes slowly. He talked in a very feeble tone.

"When did you come? Where is Vasundhara?"

"Just now. Vasundhara has gone home. She will be back in a couple of hours".

She continued showing concern, "Alok, I know what is going on in your mind. I feel that I brought you to this condition." She was sobbing.

A nurse from the hospital staff requested her to be outside as the doctor was on his rounds.

The doctor came out after examining Alok.

"Who are you?"

"A family friend. I am a nurse working in Manipal hospital. Please let me know the patient's condition".

"Oh, then it would be easy to communicate with you. He has normal blood pressure as of now. But he seems to be very weak. At first I thought he is anemic. But his blood count is normal".

"Doctor, Can I talk to you for a few minutes when you are free?"

"Why?"

"Because… I am responsible for this condition."

"What did you do?"

"I will talk to you if you could give a few minutes of your valuable time."

"Certainly. We will do anything if it can help the patient."

"Thank you Doctor," she said and went back to Alok.

She was just staring at Alok's face. He had closed his eyes. She could sense the emotional conflict within him.

"Dr. Joseph is calling you," a nurse brought her out of her melancholy.

As she entered his chamber, the Doctor said, "Take a seat. Tell me sister."

"Doctor, I have to tell you something of what happened between me and Alok."

Revathi said, "I had entered into a depression after the death of my five-year-old son. My husband refused to have any physical relations with me, since in our family, there is a strong superstition that a second pregnancy always results in the mother's death. It was under these circumstances that I met Alok, who was very impressed by my voice. He encouraged me so much that I resumed my singing. I found the voice that I had lost. We went to Mysore for a college programme. He gave a very good lecture. I fell for him just like the way a wife falls for her husband. He loved my voice. He was a great source of inspiration of the Hindola song which I sang in the college. That night we could not find any means of travel to Udupi as it was raining heavely. The roads were blocked due to rocks and trees. So we were forced to stay in a hotel. I took the initiative of having sex with him, since I was desperately in need of a child. I think he is guilty of cheating on his wife, which he is not able to express. They love each other.

I shouldn't have come in between."

"So, that is the story. You mean to say, the problem is more psychological"

"Exactly, Sir. I thought I should tell you this whole story as this might help you understand the problem of the patient."

"Thank you Revathi. I will get an appointment with our psychologist."

"One more request, Sir. I will talk to his wife and make her approach you for the psychologist's appointment".

"Surely. I saw your face this morning in the TV. They were talking of your melodious voice and your programme on YouTube, which has already got some eighty thousand hits. Now I can recollect. It has been very nice of you. Like a true catholic you have come out with the truth very boldly."

"I am a three-month pregnant with Alok's child. I want to have my child. I do not intent to break their beautiful family."

Doctor Joseph was surprised. He admired the bold resolve of the strong woman.

That night they travelled together from the hospital to Alok's house. Revathi chose to remain silent. Vasundhara was blissfully ignorant of all the incidents. She treated Revathi very courteously. She had a soft corner for her, because she was taking care of her parents. She said

"I saw rave reviews of your programme. I listened to your song. Oh! That voice is straight from the heaven."

"Thank you. But... what happened to Alok? He was a source of energy and inspired me to sing. He made me discover my voice. I was trying to get over that depression after Chistopher's death. It was Dr. Kalyani who helped me to get over that depression. Alok was sent to me by the Gods. It was he who helped me come out of my frozen heart and made me sing. I am grateful to him"

"It is very nice of you Revathi to come here all the way from Udupi inspite of your several preoccupations".

"I cannot forget Alok. He made me discover my potential".

"That night I was really anxious about you. But Alok told me that he left you in your relative's house in Koramangala.."

"Yeah." Revathi's voice sounded dishonest. But Vasundhara believed their story.

They reached home. They dined together. Vasundhara said, "Your presence has helped me a lot in de-stressing myself."

Revathi was thinking very deeply and had remained in a cloud of uncertainty. To tell the truth or continue with the false story. Finally, she gathered all her courage and said, "I am pregnant. Three-months-old."

"I am very happy. I am glad finally you and Allan made up your mind and decided to start your life all over again".

"Allan has not touched my body after my son's death".

Vasundhara was shocked.

"But... Then... by whom? Sorry. I shouldn't ask this personal question".

"I didn't go to Koramangala that night. Alok and I slept together in a hotel room".

"My God! I never expected that Alok would cheat on me to such an extent."

"I am sorry Vasundhara."

"I didn't imagine Alok was so weak-minded. It is true that we didn't have sex for a few months. That was because of my frequent visits to Udupi, my children, their problems… I never expected that Alok was so cheap. How could he exploit a helpless girl for his sexual needs? How did you allow him to have sex with you? Was it some sort of a rape or any such thing?"

"No. It was me who took the initiative of forcing him to go to a hotel room. I was really attracted to him in Udupi. I wanted him to be by my side at the beach. He was just mesmerized by my alaap and songs. We had indeed decided to remain as good friends and not love each other. But, we came close to each other knowing well that we were committing a mistake. I wanted a child. Allan refused to have any physical relations with me. They believe in his family that the first child's death is a bad omen. If a second child is born after the first child's death, they consider that the mother will die".

I really wanted to have a child. I was getting closer to Alok. He said he could not cheat on you and that he wanted to be a good father to his children, a good husband to his wife. It was me who forced him to have sex with me that night…

Now Alok is driven to this condition because of my selfishness. In my eagerness to have a child, I did not consider this aspect. It did not occur to me at all."

"Which aspect?"

"I think he is finding it increasingly difficult to reveal this incident. He is feeling guilty as he thinks this is an act of infidelity on his part. That perhaps has driven him to this mental trauma."

When Revathi finished her talking, Vasundhara was thinking of her pre-marriage days. The way she was attracted to him by his voice, the way she longed to remain in his company.

'But, was it this Alok whom I loved and married?' She questioned herself.

Revathi went on. "You have to tell the doctors about this incident. He is physically alright. All the parameters like pulse rate, sugar level and all other things are normal. He is finding it very difficult to tell you. You make him come out of that false story. The psychologist will be able to make him come out of that shell of shame and fear. You please be very kind and magnanimous to excuse both of us. I will promise you that I will get out of your sight". Revathi promised.

She continued, "I have to take care of my family. You ask Dr. Joseph to refer Alok to a psychiatrist."

Vasundhara said "I will do that,"

"What about you Revathi? Have you informed your mother-in-law?" Vasundhara asked Revathi.

"I will not inform her now. But I have to inform Sr. Clara. She is like.. and she is my mother. I have to inform Fr. Bernard. I have to face very complex situations. I am mentally prepared for all this. The thought of me becoming a mother has elevated me to a very high emotional level. I will not commit suicide. Vasundhara, I am sure I have not committed any sin. If I can get a child from an intellectual like Alok, what better thing I can ask for."

"Revathi you are no mean woman. It requires a lot of courage and confidence to tell the truth under such circumstances. As a woman I admire you. I will fully support you to become a mother. I tried to be angry with you. I cannot hate you because you are very sincere. I see honesty in your tone. I don't find fault with Alok either. When an angel from the heaven straight comes to a man and begs for love, which man can resist the temptation even against the strongest will power of restraint? I trust your words. I am very happy with your concern about my family. If you find it very difficult there, stay back in Bangalore. You can easily get a job in Bangalore. Both of you will have peace if you can at least see each other. I will help you during your maternity".

"I can get a transfer to our own hospital."

"Will Allan accept you and the child?"

"I don't know. But I am not worried about that. I have poured my heart out to you and if you have accepted my faults, that is enough. Please help Alok to come out of this trauma. I found it very difficult to see him."

She was in tears. She was sobbing continuously.

"I don't know whether I should weep for myself or for Alok's condition".

"You are a strong woman. You will overcome all these hurdles and come out successful."

"Next month, I am coming to Bangalore. An eminent musician Sandhya Rao from Chennai liked my voice. She is introducing me to a music director to sing a Tamil song. Can I stay here for a night?"

"This will be the first news I am going to give Alok when he becomes normal. We will come to the railway station or the bus stand to pick you up," Vasundhara said in a happy voice.

"We have a custom called Seemantha. The song 'ChandramuKhi, PranasaKhi' that you sang is actually filmed on a pregnant woman on this occasion. This time the YouTube will play your own song for you."

"You are very large hearted, Vasundhara. My mother died the next instant I was born. I don't know who my father was. Now I feel I have found them in you."

"Keep your mind clean and fresh. You have not committed any sin. We will welcome the child to this world. If it is going to be a girl I will take her on my lap and bring her up."

"Are you so much passionate about the girl child?"

"Of course I am. I wanted a baby girl just like you. She should be as beautiful as you are. She should sing like you."

Revathi was smiling happily. Vasundhara's motherly

affection and act of forgiveness made her forget all her sorrows.

The next morning Vasundhara asked Revathi to wear the new green saree; she had bought and slipped green bangles into her hands. She had prepared delicious dishes. They ate together. Vasundhara took Revathi in a cab.

Revathi started her journey towards Udupi in the bus. She was thinking about Vasundhara. Can a woman be so generous when it comes to an extramarital affair with her husband?

Perhaps that is why Alok said the other day, "Nobility thy name is woman".

Chapter Six

* * *

Vasundhara:

She turned the TV on. It was late night. Revathi had come like a hurricane. She had stirred up the pent up emotions in her. Vasundhara had left the children at her parent's house. She thought of disclosing this affair of her husband to her parents. She thought that this would not solve the problem. Instead, it would only aggravate it. She thought of sharing this with her close friend Uma. But, Uma is too bold and modern. She thought that she had done the right thing by treating Revathi nicely. But, she had not seen this side of Alok. May be Revathi tempted him. But, he should first become alright to confront. He should get over this situation. Inwardly, she felt happy that Alok was finding it difficult to tell the truth. She felt that relatively, Revathi was mentally stronger. She didn't think that she has committed a sin.

'Very strange', She said to herself.

The next day she left for the hospital. An appointment with Dr. Vinoda Murthy had been fixed.

She talked to Alok. Alok was slowly responding to her.

"Dr. Joseph has given me the case history. You have

actually no problems. You seem to have stressed excessively during the writing of your novel. Has it been published?" Doctor asked Alok.

Vasundhara responded on his behalf and said, "It has been accepted for publication. He has to write the last two chapters. He had gone to Mysore for a college function to deliver a lecture. After that trip, he started talking less, eating less and often complained of body pain. He had a seizure once in the house. Second time he fell down in the class."

"Did you also go with him to Mysore?"

"No, I had to attend to my father. One of his friends had been with him. She had to sing."

"Who is she? Can you ask her to come here? That will help us in our investigation".

"Sure, I will call her. She is any way coming next week. She is a nurse. She helps my parents."

Dr.Vinoda Murthy and Revathi came out of the room. Alok was still lying on the bed.

"She has a very sweet voice. My husband loves her voice. The fact of the matter is that she confessed to me that she herself tempted him to have sex with him. She advised me to take Alok to a psychiatrist."

"Then she truly loves him", the Doctor said and continued, "I will give him some psychological tests. Let us see if he can come out of the shell and reveal the truth. Then there will be a catharsis. Once he speaks out of what he has hidden inside him, he will not have these seizures. Tomorrow, we will put him on sedation. Meanwhile, you ask that girl to come over here.

"She is coming here on Monday."

"Okay. We will start the treatment from Monday. Do you have a copy of his new book?"

"I have a soft copy of that on his laptop."

"Please send it to my email i.d. What is the name

of that book?"

"Hindola"

"Oh! That is a raaga known for its melody!"

Vasundhara was staying in the hospital. Her parents had come to look after the children. Vasundhara had not yet told her parents about the affair.

Her mother told her, "Take a vow to take him to Mantralaya. Miracles have happened there."

"Alright Ma. Surely, I will take him. At least let him start talking."

She opened his laptop. She didn't remember the password. She rang up Revathi. She said,

"Revathi. As suggested by you, we met Dr. Vinoda Murthy, a psychologist referred to us by Dr. Joseph. The psychologist wants to meet you."

" Sure. We will go."

"One more thing, do you know the password of Alok's laptop?"

"Yes. Your name. Vasundhara. All in small letters."

Vasundhara opened the laptop and typed the password. She saw the file "Hindola" and sent it by mail to the psychiatrist. She felt like reading the novel. She was tired physically and mentally.

Sunday evening Revathi arrived. She had come dressed in a yellow cotton saree. She looked simple, but had dressed perfectly.

"How is Alok?"

"Thank you Revathi. Your suggestion to see the psychiatrist was a very good idea." Dr. Joseph also agreed that this was a psychological problem. Dr. Vinoda Murthy wants to read the novel."

"Do you think these novelists write their own stories," Revathi asked.

"Most of the times. Or they could be just coincidences,"

Vasundhara replied.

"Hindola started when you entered Alok's life," Vasundhara asked in a low voice.

"Vasundhara , you think I am a bad woman?" said Revathi.

"Revathi, you are a woman and women can never be bad."

They laughed heartily trying to conceal all their feelings of sadness.

The next morning they were there in Dr. Vinoda Murthy's clinic. Alok was still in St. John's hospital.

"So you are that singing nightingale." Dr. Vinoda welcomed Revathi. The doctor told her, "This is the girl Alok was trying to describe in his novel."

Revathi was looking even more beautiful than Alok had described.

"Vasundhara. Can you give us some moments?"

"I will go to the hospital. Revathi, please join me there."

"Sure."

Dr. Vinoda said, "Tell me about your affair. You are honest because you came out with the truth to Dr. Joseph. You even talked to Vasundhara." Dr. Vinoda was beyond impressed.

"Did you really love Alok? It cannot be infatuation. There is a large difference in age between you two. You were married. You were trying to come out of a depression. Dr. Kalyani helps you to come out of that. Then you see an opportunity to sleep with him and have sex with him."

"Yes doctor. Did Vasundhara tell you all this?"

"No. I read Hindola. The whole novel. Last night. Have you read the novel?"

"He asked me to read the novel after it was published. Has he described me as a bad woman?"

"No. He says a lot of good things about you and your

husband. What really worries me is the last few chapters which he has not yet written".

"Why Doctor?"

"He gets obsessed with you. With your beautiful voice. With your beautiful body. He writes about the night dress you bought that night. He talks of your supple breasts. The passionate lip to kisses and your sexual intercourses."

"Is it very vulgar?"

"On the contrary, it is a very romantic read. He comes to know of your pregnancy. That is where he has stopped writing. I think it is this point when the seizures had started and he had fallen in the class room."

"I apologise doctor. I am really.... I was unaware of all these. I have already confessed to Vasundhara. She has offered to help me during my maternity days. I didn't want this to happen to Alok."

"Nothing will happen to him. In such extramarital affairs, it is honesty and integrity that helps the patient to get over the trauma. It is a temporary mental disorder. We will give the best medical treatment. You will have to support Vasundhara".

"In what way I can help her?"

"Try to stay close to Alok only when Vasundhara is present. When he talks about your pregnancy, tell him that Vasundhara has been informed of that and she wants to bring up that child, especially, because Alok liked to have a baby girl of his own. When you can get close to him in the absence of Vasundhara, tell him that she read his whole novel. Ask him to feel free to talk to Vasundhara. Revathi, I have full faith in your judgment of things. I believe your honesty and integrity. You are true to your profession."

"Thank you Doctor. I will do anything to make Alok come out of this trauma."

Chapter 7

* * *

Revathi:

Revathi boarded the cab. She was moving towards the hospital. She briefed Vasundhara about her meeting with Dr. Vinoda Murthy. She got a call from Sandhya Rao asking her to meet at a recording studio.

Sandhya Rao seemed to be immensely happy when she saw Revathi."

"You are gorgeous." she exclaimed. Come over to Chennai on Wednesday. I will send my car to the railway station. I played your song on YouTube to Shankar Vasishta.

He said, "This is the voice for that Hindola composition. Bring her straight to me on Thursday."

I went to Chennai

I managed to locate the car and went to Sandhya's house on the day she called me. It was a nice house. She was dressed up in a plain silk saree. She told me, "You can have a shower. Come neatly dressed in a silk saree. God has given you a very beautiful face. I will give you a nice saree. Dress up neatly. These people respect women draped in sarees with flowers round nicely tied up in plaits. Shankar Vasishta is particular about dresses of female singers."

Revathi dressed up in the same manner as suggested by Sandhya.

"You are an angel. If directors see you, they may offer you a heroine's role!"

"Oh! My God. I certainly cannot act."

They went to the sound recording studio. Shankar Vasishta welcomed them. He asked her to give the Malkauns alaap.

The moment she started, Shankar closed his eyes. He listened to the entire alaap with rapt attention.

"Amazing! This is the voice I was looking for. He wrote the Tamil song in English. The lyricist helped her in the pronunciation. She sang the song for herself once. "We are going to have the recording this afternoon".

"This is Mr. Alagappan. He has written this poem for us. This is Vincent, the director of this film. He will explain the situation. Sir, please start your part of the work. I will go ahead with my orchestration".

The director explained the situation. "The heroine is deserted by her husband and she had depended totally on her father. It is a song of melancholy in which the heroine has just lost her father. He knew of her pregnancy, but did not live to see the child. She speaks to the child about how her father would have sung and made the crying child sleep. She says her father would have walked through the skies to bring the moon. He would bring the angels to decorate the child with flowers from the heavens and sing for the child. Although she could do all that, she would want to give the child all his love and seek his blessings".

Shankar came and told her, "You start the alaap with malkauns shades, which you have done in that YouTube song. This has to be followed by the song. The song expresses the joy the grandfather would have experienced while playing with his granddaughter and carries you to the other mood to say he is not there to see this. The song concludes with the mother reassuring the child that she will do all this and invokes the blessings of her father. You can see the moods of agony and ecstasy. The musical waves must oscillate between these extreme moods. Have this in your mind and start singing. The composition is made accordingly".

She practiced the song in all sincerity in a studio room. The lyricist corrected her pronunciation of a few Tamil words. Everyone felt that she had given the right expressions and carried the melancholic mood of the song. Tamil appeared to be very sweet in her voice.

The recording started. The musicians who heard her alaap were spellbound. The violinists followed her alaap softly. When she started singing, it was divine. Her voice was pristine and clear. When the song ended she gave an expression of a soft sobbing with tears in her eyes. The lyricist had tears in his eyes.

"This is a divine voice," he said. "You gave life to my words".

"Nobody asked you to give the sounds of sobbing. But it was a tremendous expression. I had not planned it. It was a great end to a melancholic song."

"You will have to make a few more trips to Chennai. I am going to book you for a few more films. I think you are working in the some hospital," Shankar asked her.

"Yes, I am a nurse in Manipal hospital, Udupi."

She rushed back to the railway station. She was curious to know about the treatment given to Alok.

She reached Bangalore late in the night. She went to Vasundhara's house. Vaasundhara was waiting for her.

"How was the day?"

"Splendid. They were very happy with my singing. I was singing without knowing the exact meaning of the words. But, I was able to carry the right mood. I will have to make a few more trips to Chennai."

The next morning, she took a bus to Udupi and came home.

The door was open. Gracey had come home.

'Oh My God! Suppose she comes to know of my pregnancy, what do I tell her?' She thought.

"Where have you been?" Gracey asked her.

"Gracey, I got a chance to sing in a Tamil film. I have sung a song for them. I will have to make a few more trips to Chennai."

"They gave me ten thousand rupees for this song. Gracey, this is for you. I seek your blessings."

Gracey looked at Revathi's stomach suspiciously, but refrained herself from talking.

That evening Revathi was getting ready with her uniform. She had the morning shift starting from the next day.

Gracey came to her room. She said, "You are looking very pretty. Are you pregnant?"

"Yes, Gracey"

"Why did Allan do this to you? We are scared of a second child after Christopher's death." Gracey said with a worried tone.

"Gracey. I don't want to lie. It was not Allan."

"What?" Gracey was shocked.

"All this happened in Mysore. You remember I had gone to a college function?"

"Are you pregnant with Alok?"

"Yes. I want a child. I can't live with these superstitions. You are living in a world of superstitions."

"Have you told Allan?"

"Why should I? He doesn't care about me. He doesn't even touch me.

I want to have a child of mine. My own…born in my womb…

If you think, I should not stay here, I will get a transfer to Bangalore."

"You better do that. We don't want to see you dying."

Next day after duty in the hospital Revathi straight went to the church. She met Sr. Clara and informed of everything that happened.

"Are you not cheating on Allan?"

"No sister. I am helping that family. I cycle every day to the hospital and Krishna uncle's house. With my salary, I could have easily bought a scooter. I have not even bought a scooter. Allan comes and promptly pays all the bills and goes away. Sometimes he sees me in the hospital and says a hello and goes away. What kind of a relationship is this? He is a dutiful son and a great elder brother to those irresponsible younger brothers. Should I go on living like this? Had Christopher been alive, I would not have bothered about all these. I took the initiative of having sex with Alok only to experience the happiness of motherhood. There was no other ulterior motive."

"But will the society accept a fatherless child?"

"Vasundhara has promised to help me. I told her everything. She wasn't angry with me. But, she said that a woman's desire for motherhood was very much justified. There was no problem from her side. But, the sad thing is her husband has entered into a state of complex depression. A psychiatrist is treating him. I pray for his good health."

"What did Gracey say?" a concerned Sr. Clara asked.

"She started blaming Allan. I told her the truth. She asked me to lease the house as she did not want to see me die."

"What are you going to do now?"

"I came to you for help and you are asking me what I am supposed to do?"

"Okay. I will tell father. Let me see what he has to say?"

"Have you told Allan?"

"What do you want me to tell him? He doesn't care for me. He doesn't even know whether I am dead or alive. He doesn't want to leave that village and his cab."

"Okay child. Take care. Look after your health. You serve the lord by healing the wounds of many people. Jesus Christ will protect you."

"You have always been there for me sister. You are everything to me. Sister, there is a good news. I sang for a Tamil film. I got ten thousand rupees. I paid the entire amount to Gracey. Next remuneration will be for you Sister."

"Give everything to me. I will keep it for the baby."

"No sister. I will look after my baby. You keep the money. Spend it happily the way you want."

"So nice of you dear."

.

The next day Revathi received a call.

"Revathi. It is Fr. Bernard talking to you. Is it the right time to talk to you?"

"Yes Father. Good afternoon Father."

"Gracey had come here. She told me the whole story. I would like to talk to you. Can you please come over here in the evening after your duty hours?"

'Gracey went to father? She is certain that she wants me to leave the house. Never mind, I am like a river whose origin is not known. I will go along with the flow,' She thought to herself. She met Fr. Bernard in the evening. He said, "This is a very complicated issue. In our family, we all believe that the first child's death is a bad omen to the family. You could have adopted a child if you were so much in need of a child. You will have to leave Udupi. You can join St. John's medical college or continue as a nurse working in that hospital. I will make the necessary arrangements. I don't want to question you regarding your right to acquire motherhood. But, that cannot happen in our family. I cannot keep you in the convent also. Everyone knows that you are not pregnant with Allan. Take this letter. You meet the administrator of St. John's hospital in Bangalore. He will make all the arrangements. May god bless you."

Revathi was taken aback at the turn of events. She said, "Atleast now, can you tell me where my grandfather is? I didn't see my mother. I will try to find out my father and help him out."

"They are good. Allan is taking care of them. You don't have to worry about them. I told you the other day that we are not supposed to reveal all that. Sr. Clara will always remain as your mother. For any help feel free to come here. When you give birth to your baby, I will certainly visit you."

"Even at that time I must not come here and visit Sr. Clara?"

"Please do not come here. We will visit you."

Revathi was sobbing. Tears rolled down her eyes. There were tears in Fr. Bernard's eyes too.

Revathi felt that she was an orphan.

"I am an orphan. I am a sinner. I killed my mother as soon as I was born. Father I am ever grateful to you. I will always look up to you whether in a crisis or a happy moment."

With a heavy heart she came back home.

"Thanks for all your help Gracey. Tomorrow, I will submit my resignation and go to Bangalore."

"Revathi, don't have any hard feelings. I am afraid of losing you. In our family, the Gods cannot accept the second child's birth after the first child's death. Since you are pregnant with someone other than our family, I only pray to God to have mercy on you and save you and the child. That cannot happen here. So, please go away and lead a happy life. If God willing, Allan and you would reunite. But, please don't break Vasundhara's family."

"Surely. Gracey."

Revathi packed all her belongings and set out for Bangalore.

She reached St John's College. She went straight to the administrator's office.

She handed over the letter to Fr. Claude Desouza.

"Yes. Fr. Bernard spoke to me last night. I will accommodate you in Nurses' quarters.

Tomorrow you report to the head nurse Sr. Matilda who will formally interview you. You will get your appointment order by tomorrow."

He called the manager on the intercom, "This is Sr. Revathi. She will join us as a nurse. You can allot a house to her in the Nurse's quarters. You hand over the keys to her."

She had to live all alone in the quarters.

'This is a new experience,' she said to herself.

She opened the door. The house was clean. She was tired and lay down on the bed. She had brought some fruits which she ate after a little rest. She was overtaken by sleep.

The next day she met the head nurse Sr. Matilda.

"Fr. Bernard sent you?"

"Yes Sister, may I please sit?"

"I am sorry. I should have asked you to sit first."

"You have come at the right time. One of our nurses just left a few days back. Since you were working in Manipal hospital, I don't think any formal interview would be required. Just fill in these forms. You can open an account in the bank which is attached to the hospital.

Revathi started working immediately. She got used to the routine quickly. Her work was same, but in a different place.

Her pace had reduced due to the pregnancy. One day while walking on the corridor, she lost her balance and was about to fall when a junior nurse came to her rescue. "Please sit down sister." She brought her a glass of water. She drank the water and thanked the student.

"What happened Revathi? You were about to lose balance and fall. That student told me." Sr. Matilda enquired.

"I was feeling giddy. But now I feel a little better."

The nurse took her hand and checked the pulse. "Are you pregnant?"

"Yes," Revathi replied.

"Which month?"

"Third month"

"Where is your husband?"

"He is somewhere in Goa. I don't want to go there. He doesn't want to come here."

"Forget about that. We are all here. You will be taken care of."

"What about you?" Revathi asked her.

"I am not yet married. I have a big family to maintain."

The mobile phone was ringing. Revathi answered the call.

"Hey. It is me Shankar Vasishta. Your song has become a super hit. It has been nominated for the best song of the year. In Chennai, you can listen to this song in every channel. Many are using your alaap as a ring tone for their mobiles. I had told you that you will have to make several trips."

"Sir, I am pregnant. I may not be able to come to Chennai very frequently. I have just joined St. John's hospital. I cannot get leave either. I cannot leave this job. I will come on all Sundays."

"Don't worry Revathi. I have three Tamil films in hand. I will arrange the flight tickets for you. I will take care of all your transportation. You just record two songs per day. I am sure you can sing atleast for one more month. There is one Kannada movie for which I will do the recording in Bangalore next month. That should not be difficult for you."

"Surely sir. I am very grateful to you for your

encouragement. It is a very big favour you have done to me."

"I really don't know who is favouring whom! Thanks for accepting my offer. You will be signing my contract for another two months. I will be paying you two lakhs excluding all transport expenses."

"Thank you Sir. I do not know whether I deserve such a huge amount."

"If you win the best singer award, you will be paid Rs one lakh per song. Already many big music directors are planning to book you. It is only after the awards are announced that you will see a large number of music directors approaching you. Next Sunday we will record two songs. One is based on your favourite, Hindola. The other is based on raag Yemen. That is a duet. You will be singing with a young boy, who also has a very melodious voice. I have planned some overlapping patterns. I will be sending you the track singer's version. I thought of recording straight from your voice. In view of your limited availability, I will do the track singing here. Practice that at home. When once you come here, we will have a few rehearsals and go for the recording"

Chapter Eight

* * *

Vasundhara:

It had been a traumatic experience for me for the past two or three weeks. The bright side of my life is that Alok has been showing a lot of improvement. He seems to be gaining strength day- after-day. Dr. Vinoda Murthy's treatment helped Alok a lot. When he came to know how Revathi was able to convince me and I respected Revathi's relationship with him, he appeared to be cheerful. When I told him that it was Revathi, who requested the doctors for a psychiatric treatment and explained the real reason for his complex depression, he said he would thank Revathi. I tried to contact Revathi even the previous day to give the good news that Alok resumed his normal work in the college. But, I could not get to her.

The mobile phone rang. She took the phone and said "Hello"

"This is Sr. Clara here. I have a news which will make you very happy. Revathi has won the best singer's award at the national level. She is in great demand. But, she goes to Chennai only on Sundays and records two songs."

"Sister, why is she not picking the phone?"

"She had some tough time. But, she is a brave girl.

As they say, when the going gets tough, the tough get going"

"What happened sister? We are not aware of anything."

"You do not know anything? When Gracey came to know of her pregnancy, she asked her to leave the house. Fr. Bernard expressed his inability to keep her in the convent. But, he helped her in getting a job at St. John's hospital, Bangalore. Now she stays at the Nurse's quarters. In the meanwhile, a music director in Chennai spotted her talent and gave a chance to sing in a Tamil film. The song was based on her favourite raag Hindola. That song became a huge hit and won her the national award. I thought I should first share this news with you, because it was Alok who made her sing."

"Sister, that's a great news. I would love to go and hug her wherever she is. She saved Alok from a mental trauma. Now she has fulfilled her ambition of becoming a singer. We are very proud of her."

"Now-a-days it is very difficult to meet her or even talk to her."

"Sister I am delighted. Please convey our best wishes to her. If I get a chance, I will personally go and thank her. Thanks for this great news."

Vasundhara was happily telling all these good things about Revathi to Alok. He said,

"She doesn't even have the courtesy to inform me. She is so ungrateful!"

"You cannot be possessive about her. In fact she saved you from the mental trauma at the cost of her own personal life. You must share her happiness and proud moments. We didn't support her during her crisis. Gracey asked her to leave the house. Fr. Bernard expressed his inability to keep her in the convent. But, of course he helped her finding a job. She has fought bravely against all these odds. It is like swimming against the direction of the flow of the river. You should congratulate her. I think you should go and personally thank her. I am also willing to come with you. Wait… I will try to contact her".

Vasundhara dialed her number. This time it was ringing.

"Hey! It's me Vasundhara. How are you Revathi? Heard a lot about you. Sr. Clara gave us the information about your winning the National award. Congratulations."

"Thank you. How is Alok? Actually I wanted to convey the news to him first."

"He is good. He has resumed going to the college. Please talk to him. He will be very happy."

"Hey. Revathi."

Revathi heard his voice after a long time. There was a mixed emotion of joy and sadness in her. She was in tears. She was finding it very difficult to speak. She composed her mind and tried to be calm.

'I should not get emotional,' she said to herself.

"Alok. I actually thought of informing you about my success first. But, I was really worried about your mental trauma. My prayers haven't failed. God has brought you back to normalcy. Alok I am happy to tell you that we both have won this award. I want you to be there in the awards ceremony...

You brought me to light. You helped me discover my voice."

"That beautiful voice is God's gift to you. Vasundhara told me about your decision to take me to a psychiatrist. It helped me to get a new life. Thanks."

"Thank you for everything. I am very busy. I am recording on Sundays too."

"Vasundhara and I will find some time to visit you. Bye."

Vasundhara

'I could not see Revathi as a girl, who had an extramarital affair with my husband. She appeared as a kindhearted woman,

an angel sent by the Gods to help me in the most critical period of my life. The way she came forward, the way she talked to me taking all the blame on her, standing by me in those difficult times was remarkable', I said to myself. This honest revelation helped me gather my strength and brought Alok from a complex psychiatric situation. All this, she did risking her own personal life. Thrown out of her house, from everybody she loved, the way she came out victorious is an inspiration for any woman....

I didn't enquire about her pregnancy. Poor girl. She must be nearly four months pregnant now. I will try to give my best when she stops going to the hospital duty and bring her home."

Vansundhara seemed to have made up her mind.

She switched on the TV. It was the national news TV channel.

"In our programme 'Achievements' today, we present a great singer, "Revathi" this evening. She is the new singing sensation whose voice has captured the entire country."

"Welcome Revathi Madam." The host introduced her.

"Thank you Sir. Please don't call me Madam. Just call me Revathi." Revathi tried to be polite.

'Revathi in a cream-coloured Mysore silk saree is looking awesome,' Vasundhara said to herself. She called Alok. He was writing the last few chapters of his novel."

They got a few minutes to talk. A few commercial advertisements were getting telecast.

"Alok. She looks gorgeous. The real moon faced girl, the soulmate, the real source of energy, the real strength of the entire mankind ... I see the real woman in her."

"You seem to be very happy."

"Aren't you?"

"Of course I am."

"Let us listen to her."

The interviewer, an elderly smart gentleman in his

immaculate suit sat in front of her. "I think this is Prof. Murthy." Alok said.

"He is a well known critic and a regular columnist in some leading English dailies."

The interview started with Prof. Murthy giving an introduction by referring to Revathi as the girl with the golden voice.

He said, "A nurse enters the film music world singing, one of the most melodious songs in the recent times. She blends the two forms of our classical music, the Hindustani and the Karnataka music, so beautifully and brings out a divine music of her own. She comes out with the beautiful Kannada song in a college function and gets nearly a hundred thousand likes in Facebook and thousands of comments by eminent musicians. She sings her first movie song for a Tamil movie and goes on to win the National award for the best singer of the year. She is Revathi from Udupi.

"Welcome Revathi," he continued to praise her.

"What was your reaction when you came to know about the award?"

"Incredible! I thought. I had immense faith in my voice. But, certainly I didn't expect this would happen."

"Tell us something about your background," the interviewer asked.

"I grew up in a convent. My mother died immediately after she gave birth to me. My grandfather brought me to the convent in Udupi.

Sr. Clara and Fr. Bernard are my protectors and virtually my parents. Sr. Clara is my mother. She is there for me at any point of time. Fr. Bernard encouraged me to study. He had put studies as the first priority. I was interested in the medical profession. I completed the nursing course. I am a qualified nurse. I have worked in Manipal hospital. Now I am at St. John's hospital, Bangalore. My Kannada teacher and my music teacher are a great source of inspiration for my musical journey. My music teacher recognized the melody in my voice. She encouraged me to sing. I used to sing in all school functions. I was a lead singer in the church choir. I enjoyed singing."

"Your song in Teresian college took you to a very high level. On YouTube, I learn that it hit one hundred thousand likes."

"Yes. I express my deepest gratitude from the bottom of my heart to Dr. Kalyani, my mentor and Prof. Alok Vyasathirtha, my well wisher. I was in a depression after losing my five-year-old son. These two great people helped me in coming out of my depression. It was Alok's idea to bring me on the college platform and sing. Actually, Alok had just substituted Dr. Kalyani to lecture on the emerging role of the modern woman. Dr. Kalyani had to go to the US to meet her son. Her journey got preponed and Alok had to donn that role. So, it was his idea that I should sing that immortal song."

"What in your opinion is the reason for that song to become such a huge hit?"

"Alok had visualized the whole song to come up in a particular manner. He is very passionate of the raag Hindola. He was writing his novel by the same name. He researched a lot on that song and that brought him to Dr. Kalyani."

"You mean to say, that it was Prof. Alok's concept that made his talk and your song such a big hit?"

"Certainly. He had heard me sing the Malkauns alaap even before he had seen my face. He wanted that to come first and the Hindola song attached to it. The musicians with the violin and the veena decorated that so nicely that it turned out to be liked by so many people. The common man enjoyed the melody and the renowned singers were appreciative of the pure music".

"Even the intellectuals, writers, thinkers have liked

it so much. How was that possible?"

"I think the credit should go to Alok. He explained the important role of women and the adaptability of the raag Hindola to this composition. His voice harmonized with the mood conveyed by the raaga."

"I think you are right. At first, I found that it was just a beautiful song sung very melodiously. But when I heard that song over and over, the whole thing looked divine."

"What about this Tamil song which went on to make you the best singer of the year?" The interviewer asked.

"This song describes the moods of the heroine, deserted by her husband on account of which she has to live with her father. He knows about her pregnancy, but dies before he could see the child. She speaks to the child about how her father would have sung and made the crying child sleep. She says her father would have walked through the skies to bring the moon. He would bring the angels to decorate the child with flowers from the heavens and sing for the child. Although he could not do all that, he gave her all his blessings.

When this song was explained to me, I was thinking of my helpless grandfather. You can just imagine his feelings at that time. My father went away on seeing that the child was a girl. I had been thinking of all these and the sobbing in the end was so spontaneous. I thought that will spoil the beauty of the song. But the director wanted to retain that. My music director was very confident that the song will be a big hit. It indeed became a big hit."

"Your sweet voice really haunts us and we feel like hearing that song again and again. Your thoughts of sadness, your own experiences have added to the creation of that melancholy. I would like to add here,

"Our sweetest songs are those of our saddest thoughts."

"Can you please sing a few lines for our viewers?"

She sang the Tamil song.

Alok said,

" She has sung that song beautifully. She deserves the award."

Vasundhara said,

"Yes, she truly deserves that. I was very happy when she spoke about you. First, she respectfully addressed you as Prof Aloknath Vyasatirtha . Then, she started calling you Alok, spontaneously showing that you are dear to her. You must call her and acknowledge her mentioning you".

"She is a celebrity now. How can I talk to her?"

The mobile phone was ringing.

Alok picked up the phone and saw Revathi's name flashing on the screen. He handed it over to Vasundhara.

"It is Revathi. May be she wants to talk to you."

"Hey. It is me Revathi. Did you see my interview on the TV?"

"Surely we did see it. You were gorgeous on the screen. Your voice, even if you are talking, it is so musical."

"Actually, I want just the three of us to have dinner tonight. I am coming in the evening from Chennai by flight. I will reach your house around 9 pm. I want to see Alok in his happy mood. Today he is refusing to leave my mind. I am longing to see him. Is it okay?"

"The pleasure is mine. I will prepare some dishes you are very fond of. We will have dinner in our house. You can sleep here tonight. You can go to your room tomorrow."

"Thank you Vasundhara. It is very nice of you."

Chapter Nine

* * *

Alok:

Revathi came home at 9 pm, it was dark .The street lights were off ~~so~~. So Alok went to get her from outside, flashing light from a torch. Her face was radiating happiness. She was beautiful. Her face looked like a bright-faced moon. Her flowing hair was raven. There was no makeup on her face. She had just a small red kumkum at the centre of the forehead. She was draped in a light yellow-coloured saree. Her long beautiful arms emerging from her sleeveless blouse beckoned Alok to embrace her. He was very controlled and restrained.

Vasundhara was inside the kitchen. Revathi embraced Alok. This time it was not sensuous. It appeared to be very friendly and warm. She thought of kissing him, but refrained from doing so. They entered the house together. Vasundhara gave her a very warm hug.

"At last the angel condescends on this poor couple."

"You really know that I am a very simple person," Revathi replied.

"Of course you are."

They had a good dinner. They enjoyed talking to

each other.

"Revathi. I think it is going to be a girl," Vasundhara said.

"How do you say that?"

" You are looking very pretty. Your face is radiating and reflecting light."

Alok was a mute spectator to the proceedings. He felt that there was a strong force of attraction drawing him to her. He went abruptly into his room and bolted from within.

The next morning, Vasundhara asked him in a soft tone, "You were feeling very uncomfortable last night? You didn't even congratulate her or talk about her interview."

"She is a big celebrity now." He said with a straight face.

"Don't have such ill feelings. She is pregnant. We should try to keep her happy always. I will go for a shower. You just talk to her and speak about her achievements.

"I am afraid I will do something wrong."

"Nothing of that sort will happen. I know about your relation now. You are not so weak mentally."

"Okay."

Vasundhara went inside the bath room for a shower.

Alok slowly entered the drawing room. Revathi was seated on the sofa. As soon as he entered the room she came close to him. She embraced him very tightly and kissed him passionately. "I want to sleep with you Alok. I want to experience the same happiness that we had in Mysore once again."

"You should not indulge in such activities hereafter." Alok said trying to hide his feelings.

"You know a pregnant woman wants her husband to be with her always."

"Don't ever think of all that. Vasundhara will be here shortly. You sit opposite to me. Talk something about your achievements."

"I wish I could be with you wherever you go. Okay. I will call you up tomorrow when you are in the college. 1 to 2 is our lunch hour. You can expect my call during that time."

"Please don't," Alok replied.

They saw Vasundhara coming out from the bathroom.

She started talking..

"What happened to your book? Is it complete?"

"It is almost complete."

"What is the end?" She asked curiously.

"I cannot reveal it to anyone. I wanted the whole novel to be read by all of you only after the publication. But all of you obtained the soft copy from my laptop. I want the end to remain as a suspense."

Vasundhara joined them. She said,

"One star is born in the musical world. I have to see the birth of a new star in the literary world. I am holding my breath."

"Relax. The world is going to wake up to see the new star shortly."

"Bye, Vasundhara. I have to go to my duty in the hospital."

The cab came in. Revathi bade good bye and entered the cab.

Alok was feeling very happy and nervous.

'My God! When she kissed me, there was a current running in my body. Fortunately, Vasundhara was inside the bathroom. Otherwise I don't know, what would have happened. Vasundhara has accepted our relation. But, I should not betray her trust. Revathi is still thinking of me and wants to continue the relation. Today, if she calls me up, I shouldn't answer the phone.' Alok was in the process of making up his mind when the phone rang.

'Yes. It is Revathi,' he said to himself.

"Hey. It is me Revathi. Can we meet this evening

near M.G road metro station?"

"Revathi, This is not correct. We should not cheat on Vasundhara."

"You have to fulfill the desire of a pregnant woman."

"Hmm"

"So, we are meeting at 5.30 pm."

Revathi was sure that he would come. She could see the desire in his eyes last night when he eagerly came out to welcome her.

The evening of the meet:

They met at the Metro railway station. Revathi was exuberant with joy. Revathi was a celebrity. Many people travelling there recognized her. They went to a coffee shop nearby.

"Revathi, you are a celebrity. They are taking photos on the camera. I am afraid, if it is streamed on YouTube or something like that, I will get into trouble."

"Nothing like that will happen. We will enjoy this moment. I am proceeding to Udupi tonight. Fr. Bernard has called me up."

"He was not even ready to keep you in the convent. So why this change of heart?"Alok asked.

"He told me that he has important information for me."

"Okay. Go on."

"Actually, I want to spend a night with you again. Can you come over to Udupi? This Sunday, there is no recording."

"I cannot do that."

"So, you don't love me?"

"I do. But the thought of cheating my wife is not acceptable to me."

"You come to Udupi. All your apprehensions will be removed. We will have some nice time."

Alok did not reply. But the thought that a beautiful woman like Revathi belonged to him, made him feel very happy.

Once he was home, he opened his laptop. He started typing. He was planning the end of the novel. 'Another four chapters', he thought.

"What will Revathi do in Udupi? What information does he have to reveal to her?"

His novel had reached a similar stage. The heroine, an orphan just like Revathi is curious to know where his father lived? She goes in search of him.

'Does Fr. Bernard know about Revathi's father? Will he give that information?'

He thought of calling her up to find out the reason, but her phone had been switched off.

The whole night he had been thinking about the end of the novel.

Chapter Ten

* * *

Revathi:

She reached Udupi the next morning after she met Alok. Fr. Bernard's phone call had disturbed her.

'Why did he call me up? He said he had an information for me.

She was sitting in Father's chambers, waiting for him.

"Hello Revathi. Thanks for coming. How are things?"

"So far, so good. Now I am not able to do the audio recordings. I have recorded eight songs so far. I have received two lakhs rupees.

I may not get leave in the hospital since I am still on probation. The administrator told me to apply for leave without pay for three months after the delivery. After the probation period he said, he would try to get the salary for the maternity leave period."

"That is fair enough. But the reason for calling you is to take a decision on our property in Panambur and Goa."

"Am I still involved in these things?"

Allan doesn't want to give you a divorce in spite of the fact that you are not living together. We thought of giving you, your share of your property. Your child will get the property in spite of the fact that the child is born to you out of an illicit affair. We respect your view that a woman has a right to motherhood. So, you might get about five acres of land. You can use it for your future."

"Okay Father. I will use it for the betterment of our family."

"You have another responsibility. Your brothers-in-law as you know are highly irresponsible. You will be their guardian. You have to make them responsible citizens. This has been at the suggestion of Gracey. But, this whole process will take a few months. She wants you to be there with her. She feels secure with you. She says she cannot depend on Allan. Allan prefers to stay in Mangalore in that village."

"I will deliver the baby in Bangalore. I will take the help of my friends. I will come over to Udupi after six months".

"Please take care of Gracey. She is getting old. I think she is having Alzheimer's disease."

"I was with her all these days. It was she who asked me to get out of the house," Revathi said.

"There seems to be some misunderstanding. I think she will come to terms with you," Fr. Bernard tried to comfort Revathi. "Here is a family falling down. We look forward to you to hold this and support it, he added."

"I will do my best. I assure you father."

Revathi was in a dilemma. She dialed Allan's number.

Allan picked the phone.

"Hey! It is me Revathi. How are you Allan?"

"I am good. How are you?"

"I am good. I want to meet you. I will come with George. I want to talk to you."

"Surely. Just give me a call before you come. I will schedule my program and wait for you. When are you due?"

"Another two months. Thank you Allan"

Revathi went to her house, that used to be. She entered Gracey's room. A fair girl was sitting.

"Are you taking care of Gracey?"

"Yes. I am Mary."

"Who brought you here?" She asked.

"George," was her reply.

Gracey tried to say something. She could hardly speak. She was in tears.

"Gracey, I met Fr. Bernard. He has told me everything. We will set things right. I will fix an appointment with a doctor. You will be alright."

Gracey pointed her fingers at Revathi's stomach."

"I am alright. I will take care. Please pray for me. Your prayers will be a great source of strength for me."

She returned to Bangalore. She thought she would take Vasundhara's support and called her up and told her about her Udupi trip. She said, "Do not think of those problems now. Just take care of your health," she said supportively.

She dialed Alok's number. She briefed him about the happenings in Udupi.

"It is really sad to know about Gracey. I had met her once when I had been to Udupi."

"Alok, I want you to come here. We will go out somewhere and talk. My mind is immersed in an ocean of problems. You have to support me. Otherwise I will be shattered."

Vasundhara and Alok came the next day. They decided to move Revathi to their house. Vasundhara said, "From now on, you are my sister. I want to see you smiling. If you can get me a baby girl I will keep it. I will bring up the baby. You go back to Udupi and try joining Allan. That is the best thing that can happen."

They went together. Vasundhara and Alok packed all her things.

"Come along. Walk carefully. You are not alone. You are carrying your child."

Vasundhara cautioned Revathi.

"I am blessed to get you like my mother. You are God's precious gift to me."

Vasundhara had made a very good room in the ground floor. She asked her sons to move to the first floor. She made a new mattress and a new cot for Revathi to make her feel comfortable. She was a very dedicated person, especially when it came to this kind of a situation.

After Revathi shifted to Alok's house, he had made a habit of coming early in the morning once to just enquire about her. He used to sit on the cot for a few minutes and go away. In the evening, he just visited her to say hello.

I want him to sit with me and talk to me. But, that is not happening. Vasundhara on the other hand, is showering all the motherly affection.

It was a Sunday. Vasundhara approached Revathi and said,

"I have to attend a function. It is the eightieth anniversary celebration of my uncle. It is an important family function and I am going with the children. Alok will be at home. He will be coming to the function later. We call it "Sahasra Chandra Darshana". A person completing eighty years would have seen one thousand full moon days. Alok will drop us and come back. He will again come at 12 Noon and we will all be back in the evening. My parents will also visit you in the evening."

Revathi was alone at home. Alok had gone with his wife and children to leave them near a convention hall which was almost twenty miles away from their house. He met his father-in-law, Rukmini, his mother-in-law and some close relatives of Vasundhara.. She had a huge family circle and Alok was liked by all of them. Alok had a good sense of humour and all cousins of Vasundhara enjoyed talking to him. They were not aware of the recent developments and were surprised when they discovered his new behavior. Vasundhara was discreet and had not informed her parents either.

Alok came back home.

"I have some writing work to do. If you want anything, please do call me," he said and was about to leave her room.

She said, "I just want you. I don't want anything else."

"Revathi. You are always in one part of my heart. I love you. You gave me a new birth."

She came close to him. She embraced him. She moved her hand through the curls of his hair. She kissed him with love. There was no sensuous feeling in her."

Alok controlled all his feelings. He just closed his eyes and remained restrained against the strongest feelings incited by her beauty and the sweet timbre of her voice.

"Say something," she said.

"What should I say? You gave your love. You surrendered your body and heart to me. You made me speak when I had lost the power to speak. You sang some the sweetest melodies in my life," he said.

"I often play your speech. Your voice mesmerizes me. I think it is a great harmony. The joyous moments of motherhood, the pleasure in that pain; you brought it back to me."

"Okay. What did Fr. Bernard tell you?" "Gracey is suffering from Alzheimer's disease. I have to take care of my family, my husband, and my brothers-in-law. He told me that he believed in my strength and appointed me as the guardian of the family."

"What about Allan?"

"Allan is looking after our lands in the village He is a hard worker. He loved Christopher very much. They all loved him. We were not fortunate to have him with us. I believe we have about forty acres of property."

"You said Allan is looking after your property."

"We have about forty acres of land. They are mostly cashew plantations. We have some rubber plantations in Mangalore. There are some agricultural lands. There are some barren lands. Allan has to keep moving. Sometimes George goes there."

"What about his extramarital affair?" Alok asked him.

" Honestly, I cannot believe that. He is very religious. He is a strong believer in God. The two brothers are also of that kind. They are irresponsible, but they are good. I remember the way they swept across the sea trying to find Christopher. Their family bondings are very strong. So, I have this task of rehabilitating these brothers. I have to first make them understand the importance of hard work. I have to counsel them to join a job."

"So, who is looking after Gracey?"

"George has brought one girl from the village. She looks just like me. She has not had a formal education. She doesn't have those niceties of a city girl.

She seemed to be polite and kind at heart. Fr. Bernard asked George to bring her."

"Okay. I am going. I have to bring Vasundhara. Bye."

After Alok drove off, Revathi sat for some time, on the sofa and retired to bed.

She was thinking of her future. She had to take care of Gracey. She felt sad for Gracey. The feelings frozen inside her heart seem to have no outlet. Sometimes they come in the form of a lifeless dull smile. That dull smile could only bring a tear in her.

'The best way to serve her', she thought, "would be to stay with her till her end. If I go with the child, may be it may cheer her up. But, she was aware of the fact that it is not Allan's child.'

She was in a deep sleep when the doorbell rang. She walked slowly and opened the door.

Krishna and Rukmini greeted Revathi.

"We came here just to see you. I had actually planned to go to Udupi straight, soon after the function. The desire to see the pregnant Revathi brought us here."

"Thank you Ma'am. I am fortunate to have such a wonderful sister like Vasundhara."

"You have to promise one thing. You will have to come back to Udupi, after the child is born. Vasundhara told everything. We want our daughter to be happy. Please, for heaven's sake, don't continue this affair with Alok."

"No. I have lots of work to do in Udupi. I am definitely taking back my child away. I am planning to settle down in Mangalore or Goa."

"You are a nurse. You can get a job anywhere."

"Of course."

"Bye then."

Krishna was observing all the proceedings. He remembered how she used to ride her bicycle, and come all the way.

"I am ever grateful to you my child. You were a source of big help in my post surgery days. If I can walk today, it is because of you," he said. You moved happily in our house making those beautiful alaaps. Your sweet voice was so divine. I was told that you are now a big celebrity. I saw you on the TV in an interview. I read an article in The Times of India about you. I feel very proud of you."

"Thank you. I was fortunate to serve you."

"Bye then. Have a safe delivery. Take care."

" I seek your blessings. Please pray for me."

They took leave of Revathi.

As the car moved away, Vasundhara waved her hands. Revathi slowly waved her hands.

Revathi was thinking of her days in Udupi. Her favourite cycle could take her wherever she wanted. That inanimate object seemed to know her mind and moved accordingly; the Malpe beach where she could sit and hum. The sea waves seemed to dance in the cool evening softly in resonance with her tune.

Suddenly those waves came in a fury making thunderous sounds. Christopher enjoyed running in the waves. She closed her eyes.

"Mom, she is sleeping"

Vasundhara's son Apoorva seemed to be telling his mother.

She opened her eyes. Apoorva enjoyed staying with Revathi.

"Please sing a song for me," he asked in a very polite tone.

"Apoorva . Come here. Don't disturb her," Vasundhara called her son.

"She is going to sing a song for me."

"Not now. Tomorrow. After you come back from the school," Revathi pacified him.

Revathi remembered the way Christopher used to pester her to sing the nursery rhymes. He liked singing with Revathi. He enjoyed the lullabies which would put him to sleep."

"Revathi, we have to go to the hospital at 11 AM. Have a shower. Get dressed up. We still have three hours left. Have your breakfast.

"Why are you in tears?"

"Nothing …She tried to bring a pale smile forcibly. Yeah, I will.."

"These days you have to keep yourself very happy. If you are sad, the child inside your womb will weep with you."

"No, it was just … You are so kind to me. I shouldn't

have cheated on you. I am very sorry. When Apoorva talked to me, I felt like, I was talking to Christopher."

"Revathi. This is not the time to cry or become emotional and think of sad things. This is the phase of a motherhood which you should enjoy. Forget about the past and think that you are welcoming your first child. I know... it is very difficult. You must think that Christopher is coming back to you."

"Thank you Vasundhara. You are a great healer."

Vasundhara said, "I have fixed up an appointment in Chandra nursing home. I have briefed her about you. She is very friendly."

They were travelling in the car. Revathi asked, "Who is the driver?"

"Yes. I was able to find Shivu. He was referred to me by your husband Allan. He had rang up. I was at the function. I discovered that I had carried your phone, as both the phones look identical.

I told him about the change of phone. He enquired about your general health condition. I requested him to find a driver. Within fifteen minutes, he called me back and gave Shivu's number. Shivu will be with us hereafter."

"What about Alok?"

"He rides to the college in his motor bike."

They went inside the nursing home.

"I am Dr. Bharathi. I will take care of you from now on".

Dr. Bharathi, a middle-aged woman seemed to be happy on seeing Revathi. I saw your interview. Your voice is very melodious.

"Thank you doctor."

The doctor was doing the checkup simultaneously.

"The baby has grown very well."

"Is it a boy or a girl?"

"In India, gender determination tests are not done.

In some of our villages, they resort to all evil practices. If they come to know that the child is going to be a girl, they force the woman to abortions which results in the death of the woman. So, the government has banned gender determination tests in India," she told Revathi not knowing that she was a nurse herself. Vasundhara listened quietly.

"Take care. I expect that you will start getting pains next week. The moment it starts, get admitted. Even otherwise, you get admitted next Thursday."

"Thank you doctor"

Vasundhara was telling Revathi,

"I have taken some vows. After you reach Udupi, I have to fulfill all those."

The next Thursday Revathi got admitted in the hospital. The delivery of the girl child was normal. Vasundhara seemed to be devoted in her work. Most of the time, she used to stay with Revathi.

She said, "The girl is born on Friday. She is like goddess Lakshmi. She will bring luck to our family. Apoorva and Adithya are jumping in the house with joy. They want to come here to see their little sister."

"Please bring them. I want to see them." Revathi said.

"Okay. Bye. Alok will be here shortly."

Chapter Eleven

* * *

Revathi:

The way Vaṣuṇdhara was looking after her made Revathi think that she should hereafter be very good to her. She tried to rewind all the incidents. She was trying to introspect everything. She said to herself, 'My desire of motherhood is fulfilled. I have given my body and love to a learned cultured person like Alok. I have not resorted to an illicit relationship with a cheap person. I am not anybody's mistress. I am not a whore selling my body. Of course, it was me who forced Alok to have the sexual intercourse that night in Mysore. It was the love of music that brought us together. It is the raag Hindola that brought us close together. The melody of this raaga has flown through my mind, body and through the nerves. When I sit back and sing for myself, the nerves get excited. Sometimes, they are in resonance with the vibrations of my joyous feelings and sometimes the sad feelings. There is a feeling of dedication, a feeling of surrender that makes me help see God. Music has made me see light at the end of the darkness as if I am travelling through a tunnel. I feel like living again when the future appears dark. If I have to die, I want to live again. With Alok coming in to my life, I feel that I have achieved everything. Initially, I tried to be possessive about him. I wanted him to be mine. I thought of asking him to divorce Vasundhara. I dreamt of a small house just for the two of us. I wanted to have a small family of my own. It was pure love without any adulterated feelings for him. His voice is something which can attract any woman. His views about woman, the way he expresses concern, the way he respects the feelings of others makes him a complete man. Allan lacks all these qualities. He has no emotions. But, when Christopher died, he tried to support me to overcome my grief. I could not even think of my anger about his second family in Panambur. I just leaned on his shoulders.

Vasundhara is an angel that has descended from the heavens according to me. She respected my desire of becoming a mother. In spite of the fact that I became pregnant by Alok, she stood by my side like my mother.

"Hey, how are you?"Alok's voice made her open her eyes.

"Were you sleeping?" He asked her.

"Not really. Just like that…I am thinking about the past incidents. I was just thanking Vasundhara in my mind from the bottom of my heart."

"The child resembles you. The first time I saw your face, when you opened the door." He took the child his arms. He kissed the child on her forehead very softly.

"Thank you Alok for bringing this wonderful moment for me," Revathi said.

"You still love me?"

"Of course, I do. But now you are not a lover. You are the father of my child."

"I have to go. Bye... Then.. Take care."

"Wait. Have you thought of any name for the child?"

"I think you, as a mother, should have that privilege."

"I thought of asking Vasundhara," Revathi said.

"That would be great."

Vasundhara came in the afternoon. She had brought lunch for Revathi."

"Vasundhara. I want you to name the child."

"I have Apoorva and Adithya at home. She will be Ananya. The word Ananya means something unique. This child is unique in many ways. She is born to a celebrity."

"So, she belongs to you," Revathi said.

"Of course. Do you remember the promise you had made. Ananya belongs to me. I will bring her up in my own way. She will be a beautiful musician like her mother and a teacher like her father."

"So, what should I do?

"You have lots of things to do. You have your family commitments."

Revathi thought that it would be better to leave the child with Vasundhara. Ananya would have Alok as her father and Vasundhara as a great mother.

She was feeding the baby. She was feeling a sense of excitement, a sense of fulfillment. The mother in her made her sing the sweetest tone. Without her knowledge, she was humming her some beautiful lullabies.

Six months later...

The mobile phone bell was ringing. George had called her up.

"Hey Revathi. It is me, George."

"George, What a surprise? How are you?"

"I am fine. You will have to come to Udupi by this evening. Allan is coming from Goa. Fr Bernard and our Mangalore uncle, all are coming. Joseph is bringing Gracey. We have to sign in the court. We will get the properties registered in our respective names. You will get your share."

"So, everything is settled finally… How is Gracey?"

"It is just a matter of a few weeks. The doctors are giving the best possible treatment. They said there is no point in keeping her in the hospital. Alzheimer's disease cannot be cured. We have brought her home.

"Okay". Revathi responded.

"We are going by flight to Mangalore. Allan will bring his cab to the airport. We will then go to Udupi. Allan has asked me to tell you to bring the child. He said that Gracey wanted to see the child once, before she died."

"Okay." Tears rolled down from her eyes.

George replied,, " Don't be emotional. We have to face the situation."

George took the address. He was there at Alok's house in the afternoon itself. Vasundhara served them tea.

They reached the airport. George never allowed Revathi to carry the baby. He held the baby all along and was very excited by holding the baby.

They arrived at the Mangalore airport where Allan was waiting for them.

George said to Allan,

"I will drive. You both sit at the back. He went to the parking lot.

Revathi said, "Hi Allan. How are you?

"So, this is the celebrity baby." She pressed his hand gently and tried to control her sobbing.

"I understand the emotional battle you are facing. I was also fighting a battle within me."

George brought the cab. They started driving to Udupi.

They were in their house within thirty minutes.

Revathi went inside her house. She saw Gracey sleeping on a bed. She was in tears. Her eyes spoke more than her words. "I will be here Gracey. I am not going anywhere. You are a very kind person. I know how much you love me.

I love you Gracey". She could not control her feelings. She said sobbing uncontrollably.

Allan said, "Go and have your dinner."

George was talking to Mary intimately. She said to herself, 'They might be loving each other.'

The next morning, they were there in the court. The lawyer briefed every one, the share of their property.

The court work was over. Fr. Bernard talked to Revathi.

"How are you my child?"

"I am fine. How are you Father?"

"I am as fine as I could be at this age and as my health permits. Where is your child?"

"I have left her at home. Mary is looking after her."

"Yes. She is in the right place."

Allan called all of them. He said, "Let us go home."

They went home. They had lunch together.

Next morning when Gracey opened her eyes, Allan took the child in his arms and placed the child on Gracey's shoulders. There was a tear in her eye when her eye got fixed at Allan. Allen shouted and called Revathi.

"Revathi, something has happened to Mom."

Revathi came running. She forcibly opened her eyes. She counted the pulse rate.

She said, "She is no more".

Revathi sobbed uncontrollably. Everyone was weeping. George rang up to Father Bernard

"Father, she is no more."

They arranged for a funeral service.

Revathi came to the lectern. She was dressed elegantly to suit the sad moment. She gave a reading from the bible. Then she sang the poem in a very low voice.

We Remember Her

When we are weary and in need of strength,
When we are lost and sick at heart,
We remember her.
When we have a joy we crave to share
When we have decisions that are difficult to make
When we have achievements that are based on her
We remember her.
At the blowing of the wind and in the chill of winter
At the opening of the buds and in the rebirth of spring,
We remember her.
At the blueness of the skies and in the warmth of summer
At the rustling of the leaves and in the beauty of autumn,
We remember her.
At the rising of the sun and at its setting,
We remember her.
As long as we live, she too will live
For she is now a part of us,
As we remember her.

There was silence everywhere. It appeared as if an angel had come and consoled them.

They returned home. The mourning silence was broken by Ananya's loud crying.

"I have to go back to Goa tonight." Allan announced.

"Why? Is work that important for you?"

"Not exactly. I have to talk to you regarding certain unknown facts regarding my family, myself."

"Is this the time for all this?" Revathi asked with irritation in her voice.

"You know why Fr. Bernard asked you to be the guardian of this property? It is not that he doesn't trust me."

"He told me you are a workaholic and had no time for these things," Revathi informed.

"That is not the truth," Allan protested.

"Then what is the truth?", Revathi asked.

"I am not a Desouza. I am born to my Gracey out of her first husband. But they brought me up keeping all these in dark. Gracey didn't want any share in the property owned by the Desouza family to be given to me. Whatever you and I have received now it is all Fr. Bernards's. When you see the documents you will come to know," Allan informed.

Allan

The Goa trip was about to begin. I was in a deep pensive mood. I was thinking about Gracey. I came to know about my real father through my uncle staying in Mangalore. During Gracey's hospital days, Father had spoken to me once.

"Gracey's husband Lawrence Desouza is not your father. You were born to Gracey out of a premarital affair Gracey had. I have to tell you this now. Your father is very sick and is staying in Goa. You will have to go there."

Allan was thinking to recollect why Father Bernard called him every month and asked him to take care of this family and the village watchman. He thought he would see this time, his father properly and serve him in all sincerity.

But, who is this watchman in Panambur? Why was Father so kind to him? Why had he taken it as if it was his personal responsibility to protect these families? Why did he choose me to assist these families?

'There are many questions which are unanswered. How do I find answers to all these questions? It is like tracing the origins of a river,' Allan said to himself.

Allan went straight to Goa to meet his father. He saw his father for the first time. His father was a very tall person.

He was angry with this irresponsible person. But, his feeling of anger changed because it was not him that deserted his mother. His mother left him because she could not adjust to the standard of living that this man could provide her. He just went near him and held his hand.

"I am your son Allan Desouza. Sorry, I am not a Desouza. By the way who are you? What is your name?"

"I am a fisherman settled in Goa. Gracey got married to me in her youth. Unfortunately, I did not prove to be a good husband to her. I was a drunkard. Once I brought a girl to my home and slept with her. Gracey requested me to stop all these. But, I did not give heed to her words. Gracey left me. I married that girl. She died recently.

I went to Udupi to see Gracey. But, I didn't have any clue. I went to the church. I made a confession to Fr. Bernard. He was aware of all these events. You were coming here every month to help us. Fr. Bernard had asked me not to divulge the fact that I am your real father. He admitted me to a hospital. This is my daughter Alice. Now she is looking after me. Now she is my mother".

"Sorry to know about your mother's death. Please accept my hearty condolences," Alice said.

"Are you not sorry about losing your wife?" Allan asked his father.

"Of course, I am. But I could not provide her a decent standard of living. It was quite obvious that she chose a more civilized family man. Lawrence was a rich person. Gracey could not tolerate my ways of living. She deserted me and went to him. He accepted you as his son.

He looked at the teen-aged girl.

He said. "Alice, I am your brother. You can tell me about all your needs and desires. I will take care of you. I will get you married to a boy of your choice. Which class are you studying?"

"I have just passed my eleventh. I have secured the first rank in the college in my class."

"What do you want to study?"

"I want to study medicine. My teachers are very confident that I can do well in my twelfth examination."

"If you want to join tuition classes, do so."

"They are quite expensive"

"Never mind. I am here to fulfill every good and reasonable desire of yours."

"Thank you. I will concentrate on my studies."

Allan discovered that he had a new direction to move on in his life. 'I will work for my father and my sister. They need help.' He had made a firm determination.

Chapter Twelve

* * *

Revathi:

It is nearly three months since Gracey left us. My world has been confined to these two young gentlemen. After a lot of persuasions and prodding, they seem to be coming to grips with the situation. I could make out the way George was trying to find every opportunity to meet Mary, hug her, kiss her, embrace her. Once they were caught unaware, by me. I just acted as if I didn't see them.

We could sell a portion of our land. George wanted to own a cab and drive. I made sure that he obtained the license. He was a very active person. He didn't have the capacity to take a decision on his own. He always acted on impulse. Joseph on the other hand was naïve. He refused to go to college. He was twenty-one. He wanted to be a musician. I asked him to join guitar classes and bought him a guitar. I begged him to take up a job. He is now going to computer classes and wants to do courses there.

I thought of meeting Alok. Would he be interested in seeing me? Would he be coming to see the child?

She took the cell phone and dialed his number.

"Hey, It is me Revathi? How are you?"

"Hey.... Long time. Three months... How is my little daughter? "

"You don't seem to think about the mother of your daughter?"

"Of course I do. But there are certain bounds of decorum. You are someone's wife. You are virtually the head of a family."

"Come on. Even today I think of sitting with you on the sands here on this seashore. I want you to recite a romantic poem, explain the meaning of the lines, the feelings carried by the words."

"Then come to my poetry class."

"No. I don't want to be like Vasundhara. I want you to come here just for me. I am very possessive about these things. Now that I have fixed all the things in their place, I want you to spend some time with me."

"I am afraid that may not be possible. But, I too cannot help dreaming about the days you are talking about."

"How is Vasundhara? Convey my regards to her."

"She will be coming there to Udupi to see her parents. Next month I suppose."

"The whole of next month, I will be in Chennai. I have a heavy schedule of work. I have signed for five films. I am coming to Bangalore also. At last, I have got a chance to sing in a Kannada film."

"That is great."

"How about your book?".

"I have finalized the last chapter. I had a meeting with the editorial team. They have suggested a few changes. I have to incorporate them and then it will get printed. They have a plan to hold a launching event. You will be singing for me."

"Of course, I will. It is as important to me as my

child's birth."

"It is very nice of you."

Revathi rang up Vasundhara's number.

"Vasundhara, I need a favour from you. I am going to Chennai for about three months. I have signed contracts for a few films. I am giving concerts in three or four places. They have already booked my programmes. You will have to take care of my baby for about three months."

"Sure. I have told that I will be bringing her up."

I was very sure that Vasundhara would help me. I started practicing. I formed a team of my own musicians. I had a mrudanga vidwan, a violinist, a flutist, a sitar player, etc. They were happy to accompany me.

I really enjoyed the practice sessions. Mary was a source of big help. She seemed to enjoy our sessions.

At the end of one month, we were ready. We set out for our Chennai journey.

With the help of Shankar Vasishta, we hired a small house.

I had a hectic work schedule. The joy of singing had returned to me. I was moving from one recording studio to another. I was overwhelmed with the response I received everywhere.

The concerts in which I sang, the Thyagaraja kirtanas became very famous. I used to sing a Marathi abhhang in praise of Lord Vithala. This proved to be a hit with a very large participation from the audience and their loud singing. The Kannada devotional songs became a huge hit. I used to sing an ugabhoga evert time and sing a related devara naama.

It was a concert in Triplicane in one of the temples. As I got down from the dais, an elderly person came to me. He said,

"Can you give me a few minutes madam?"

"Yes, sir."

"Are you from Mysore? "

"No sir. I am from Udupi. Why are you asking me this question?"

"We are from Mysore. I am a retired university professor in Kannada. We recently lost our son in the US in an accident. My daughter-in-law is pregnant. She is staying with us. She has lost all interest in life. In some YouTube programme she saw you and heard your Hindola composition about the importance of womanhood. From then on, we are able to see some smile on her face. Yesterday, she booked tickets to attend this function for all of us. Today, I thought I will come and thank you."

"This is a very kind gesture on your part. An elderly person of your caliber coming down here and acknowledging, I consider it a great honour. Where is your daughter? Let me meet her."

"I am very grateful to you Madam."

"Sir, please don't call me Madam. You can call me Revathi. I am very thankful to you," She bent and touched his feet.

"May you live for a very long time. Let your voice also live in this pristine, clear melodious form."

"Thank you Sir."

"I am the secretary of an association in Bangalore. We conduct the Ramothsava every year. If you give your consent and your available date, I will book a programme. We will try to pay whatever you charge."

"Sir, I am waiting eagerly to get a chance to sing in Bangalore. You don't have to pay me any big amount. You are very kind to me.

I want to know why you have come to Chennai."

"We came here just for your programme. My daughter-in-law is a software engineer working in Bangalore. I have found her often listening to your songs. She is very fond of your aalaaps. At home she plays this in her music system and tries to sing with you."

"Oh! That is a great gift to me from God. Sir, I will come to your house once. I want to meet your daughter-in-law."

"I am extremely grateful to you. It is like goddess Saraswathi coming down to give darshan to her devotees. She is right now in Bangalore. Can I take the liberty of booking a programme in Bangalore for this Ramanavami programme."

"Certainly."

"Please give me your cellphone number".

She finished her three months schedule of work. She was able to make some good money. After she returned to Bangalore, she went straight to Vasundhara's house.

"Did she trouble you?" She took her child in her arms.

"If this is what trouble is, I would like to get troubled very frequently," Vasundhara laughed.

"How was your stay in Chennai?"

"They love music and especially the classical music. There was a big response everywhere. I could make some money."

She replied after a pause, "I am going to Udupi tomorrow. I am in dark about those brothers of mine. Allan has not called me up even once. I tried to contact him. But his phone is switched off."

"Don't worry. Things will be alright. You have that strength to resolve any complex problem."

"Where is Alok?"

"He has gone to college. He is eagerly waiting for the publishing of his book."

"I am sure, it is going to be a great novel."

"Let us wait and see."

Alok arrived in the evening.

"So, how did it go."

"Good. The audience response was excellent. A

Kannada professor from Mysore University had all the way come to Chennai for my concert."

"That is great. What else can you ask for? "

"I owe every success of mine to you. You brought life in my dark world. It was a rebirth for me."

"If I start reciprocating it, I can give a lecture on your help. Hereafter, we are just good friends. "

'Just good friends...I still love you Alok,' Revathi said to herself.

She left for Mangalore by flight. When she arrived at the airport, she saw Allan helping an old man to board the cab.

Allan came running towards Revathi.

"Come along. It has been long. I would like to spend a little time with your daughter and my brothers," Allan said excitedly.

"But you have a passenger."

"Never mind. I will request him. I have to drop him in Kinnigoli. We will then proceed to Udupi."

"Sir, this is my wife Revathi. We will be going to Udupi. If you permit, can I bring her in the cab. She will sit in the front seat."

"Surely. You can sit in the backseat. You have a small child."

He got down and sat in the front seat.

They moved on. Revathi was enjoying the cool breeze. She rememberd the days when she used to travel frequently between Mangalore and Udupi with Sr. Clara. The elderly gentleman got down near his house. Allan got down and helped him to lift his suitcase.

"Thank you," he said.

"I don't' think I have to charge you. You permitted me to bring my wife."

"No. No. That is not fair. You take your regular fare."

"Thank you, sir."

Allan asked Revathi to come to the front seat. He said,

"I think it has been years. I don't remember the two of us, just the two of us travelling together."

"We never did. After Christopher's death, I don't think we have ever sat for a couple of hours and talked together."

"Shall I stop the car. Can we sit together under the shade of that tree and talk for a while?"

"Sure. We will."

"I have been following your story. How did you become a star singer?"

"I think you know the whole story including the birth of this child. Were you not upset when you came to know about my pregnancy?"

"To be honest, I was upset. It was an emotional turmoil. We could have raised a family of our own. I was going through an emotional crisis in my life. I came to know about my real father only when Gracey got to suffer from dementia. I was meeting my sick father every month without knowing who he was. Fr. Bernard had kept it a guarded secret. He didn't want George and Joseph to know about my origin. Even today, they are not aware of this fact. He didn't tell me anything. He feared that I would run away. In spite of being a priest, he is attached to his family. He believes in strong family bonding. When Fr. Bernard told me that my brothers would get all the property and I was not going to have any share, I was shocked. Am I a prodigal son? The greatest blow to my heart was the revelation that I am not a Desouza originally. I was shattered. Fr. Bernard consoled me. He said, this was destiny: and that I have to face the reality. But, he could not take a cruel decision like the way Gracey did. Because, he brought me up. He said I gave a new life to an orphan girl by marrying her. He wept a lot when he heard of the death of our son. It is said, 'Putra shokam nirantaram". The death of one's son is something which can never be forgotten. It is eternal. I have counseled so many members of our church in such situations. Even today, tears roll down when I think of Christopher's death. I wanted all my property to go to you."

"I shouldn't have done this to you Allan," Revathi spoke in a sad tone.

"But, the birth of this child made me forget all these. I didn't get angry. It is of course your right to become a mother. But, I have grown up in this atmosphere. I thought of giving you a divorce."

"You wanted to marry that girl in Goa."

"Which girl are you talking about?"

"She ditched you?"

"You want to know the truth?"

"Let the truth come out. I would like to hear from the horse's mouth."

"This is the story given to me by Dominic uncle who stays in Mangalore. He was the first to receive you when you entered our church as a ten day old infant."

He went on…

"Demonic uncle told me that your grandfather came after fifteen years. This time he had brought Mary who looked just like you. Fr. Bernard didn't want you to know that you were an orphan. Sr. Clara took the responsibility of bringing you up and that is how you became Reena. But your Kannada teacher entered your name as Revathi. Father didn't object to it.

Mary told me that you are her first cousin."

"But, what about this woman with whom you are supposed to be living in Goa?."

"I will tell you on a suitable occasion…

Let me tell you one thing. I haven't slept with any woman after my son's death.

Come … We will move on…"

After an hour's drive, they had reached Udupi.

Revathi was curious to know about her grandfather. She thought Mary could give some information. She thought of meeting her grandfather first and then her father.

That afternoon, there was no one at home. Mary was packing her things. Revathi asked her.

"Where are you going?"

"George is taking me back to Mangalore. Why?"

"My father stays there."

She was shocked. She decided impulsively.

"I am also coming with you."

George came in the evening. He was surprised at Revathi's sudden decision to visit Mangalore. He wanted to spend some time with Mary. He didn't have the courage to question Revathi's decision. The three of them were travelling in the car. The ten-month- old child was a mute spectator oblivious to all these events happening around her.

George drove straight to Mangalore. He drove to Panambur.

"This is a major port for Karnataka. I love this place. As a boy I remember the days we were visiting Dominic uncle's house situated close to the beach. I enjoyed playing in the sea waves. But, that beautiful atmosphere is missing now. Since, we are close to Surathkal, many technology centers are opening up. We have about twenty acres of land very close to the beach. Mary's father looks after that."

Revathi said,

"This is a beautiful place. Thank you George for bringing me here."

They went inside a small house. An old man welcomed them.

Mary introduced Revathi to the old man.

"Uncle, please let me know whether you know something about my father. Allan told me that Mary is my first cousin." Revathi was curious to unravel the mystery.

"Mary, prepare some tea for all of us. Bring some milk for the baby."

Chinnappan started unfolding the untold story of Revathi's birth which was kept highly confidential by Fr. Bernard, Sr. Clara and Allan.

Chapter Thirteen

* * *

Chinnappan:

Your mother was really very beautiful. She used to sing all the songs in her own way. She didn't have any training. Nobody taught her. She had a very melodious voice. Your father, Velu, was an actor. He acted in dramas in a small theater group. They used to do dramas during late nights. They used to travel from one village to another. It was in one such drama, he lured your mother, Valli, who was then a seventeen- year- old, beautiful girl. She was very innocent. Your father made false promises to your mother. She listened to him and one day ran away from her home to live with him. He took her to his village. He tied a mangalasutra round her neck in a temple. She lived with him for a few months.

There was an acute drought during that time. There was no rain. These villagers, who mainly depend on the rains, were frustrated. They started migrating towards the neighbouring cities. In such situations, these artists would naturally have no job! The company asked them to go back to their respective villages. Velu didn't have a face to come back. He just deserted her and went away to some place. Valli didn't have the courage to go come back to her house. She was afraid of meeting her father. He was my elder brother. She came to our house walking nearly ten miles in two days. She was pregnant with you at that time. My wife was Valli's mother's younger sister. We took Valli to your grandfather's house.

Your grandfather Varadaraja was very happy on seeing your mother. But, when he came to know that Valli was pregnant, he slapped her in a fit of anger. We caught hold of him and pacified him. Then of course, he started taking care caring of for her and looked after her.

The rain God was kind to us. It started raining after a few months. Your grandfather went in search of Velu. But, he could not be traced.

When Valli got her pains, we admitted her in the government hospital. The doctors could save you. But, they could not save Valli.

Your father came after he got to know of your mother's death. He was pestering Varada for money. He threatened to take away his child if no money was paid to him. But, Varadaraja did not like the idea of sending the child with him. One of his friends suggested him to take you and leave you in an orphanage. They gave the address of this church in Udupi.

Your father returned after one year. He had no money by then. One day, when there was no body at home, he raped my daughter. My daughter also committed the mistake of encouraging the advances made to her. I thought of giving my daughter in marriage to him. I sold my small piece of agricultural land and gave it to him. He took the money and went away, never to return. I told my elder brother Chinnappan about this incident. He took us to Fr. Bernard. Father was in search of a family who could settle down in the village in Panambur. He asked me to go to Panambur and look after this land. Since then, I have been loyal to him and have been living here peacefully. George comes here frequently and helps us. Your husband Allan comes here every month. He promptly hands over the monthly salary.

I had a strong desire to see you. Dominic Sir told me that you married Allan. You look so beautiful. You are just like your mother. I heard that you have become a great singer. Mary told me that you sing in films also. Your father also used to sign during his days. His singing and acting in the dramas attracted huge crowds. Unfortunately, your mother is not here to see your achievements. But, she is always seeing you from the heaven. She is blessing you.

After Chinnappan finished his story, Revathi asked him,

"Chinnappan thatha, do you have my mother's photo by any chance?"

"There is an old photo in which the two sisters are together. They were very good friends."

He took out an old photo from his trunk and gave it to her.

"The one on the right with that perfect circle face and wide eyes is your mother. When you entered our house, I thought it was Valli who entered our house."

Revathi looked at her mother's face admiringly. "She is more beautiful than me".

"Can I have this photo please? Or else I will take it home, make a copy and send the original through George."

"Okay, my dear child," Hhe replied gladly.

"May God be with you. I hear many good things about you. Allan is very proud of you. Everybody in this village knows that you are a great singer."

"Do you know anything about my father?"

"You ask Varadaraja. Mary write down Varadaraja's address and give it to Revathi. You show this photo to him. He is very old. He might know about your father's whereabouts."

"I will take your leave Chinnappan thatha."

"George, shall we go?"

Mary, we are now closer. We know each other.

Thatha, I want a favour from you. I want to get Mary wedded to George".

George and Mary looked at each other expressing happiness through their eyes. They thanked Revathi for this initiative. As George was driving,

"Reena , Tthank you very much."

"George, Ppromise me one thing. You will never hurt Mary for any reason. She is an innocent unfortunate child. We have to give her the best."

"I promise you Reena."

They were proceeding towards Udupi. Revathi texted Alok. 'I will talk to you on the skype. Keep your laptop on.'

'Sure'. The reply was almost instantaneous.

They reached Udupi late in the evening.

George said, "It is already three in the afternoon. We will have lunch here in some hotel."

"Sure. I am a strict vegetarian"

"So, you think I eat fish?" George lightened the mood.

They had lunch in a good hotel. They went home bound.

Revathi spoke to Allan on the phone. He thanked Revathi for taking a good decision. Revathi spoke about her father. She said, "I will trace him down. I will ask him if he is a man or an animal. For money's sake he had tortured my grandfather. He has made their lives miserable. I feel like shooting him in his temple, even if it means me going to prison."

"Don't talk anything emotionally. Please remember, discretion is the better part of valour or uncontrolled emotions."

"I never knew he could be so cruel. How unfortunate it is that he happens to be my father!"

"Don't generalize things and come to a conclusion. You have to hear his story also."

"I don't want to know anything about him. Let him die."

She could not sleep that night peacefully. The cruel face of her father harassing her grandfather and the gullible sisters, were passing through her mind.

'Father forgive them for they know not what they are doing....

This not for that person, my father,'

Revathi said to herself.

Joseph came home late at night,

"Joseph. You will have to come home a little early from tomorrow. You can't expect me to wait late at night"

"Sorry Reena. I had a discussion with a business partner. It went on till for a long time. From tomorrow, I will be early."

"What business are you trying to set up?"

"I want to build a five star hotel. Today, I had a meeting with a builder. He said that I would have to get a land on the beach side and they would build the hotel for us. They would find a reputed company to run the hotel."

"They will have the land in their name? What are you going to gain from this proposal?", Revathi asked.

"As an initial advance, I will be getting five lakh rupees," Joseph informed.

"Ask them to give that first," Revathi said being the more experienced one.

"They will be giving it as soon as the registration is done."

"When once the property is registered in the name of the company you will not be able to recover anything from them."

"Never. He is my close friend. He can never cheat me."

"In business, friendship and relationships are not the factors that work. It is sheer business acumen that works. You lack that. Tell your friend that it is not possible."

"Gracey did not trust me. I thought at least you would trust me," said Joseph almost raising his voice.

"Joseph, I have confidence in your ability. But you are gullible. You can be cheated easily. I want you to work like your brothers."

"I don't want to drive a cab like Allan and George."

"Then what do you want to do?"

"I want to do something of my own. I want to have a company of my own. May be an audio recording company or some software business."

"First, be clear about what you want to do? Also, try to understand what you can do? There is no point in simply dreaming."

"I don't think Gracey is dead. You are speaking her words."

"I know that you are a very good person. I know that you have a strong will power. I believe in your capabilities. Something in me tells me that you are going to be a very great achiever. I want you to channalise your energy and thoughts into something productive."

"What do you want me to do?"

"First, you join a computer course. I know that you are very much interested in computers. Do some diploma. Then I will finance you. You can open a small company. We will approach Krishna. He is very influential. We will try to establish some contacts and try to procure some orders."

"Reena, you are like your music. You are very sweet. Without hurting me, you have convinced me that I am taking a wrong step. I will follow your advice," Joseph understood what Revathi was trying to do without too many arguments.

I am going to Bangalore tomorrow in the evening. I

have a tight schedule of recordings. You have to join a computer course. I will be back here after three months. By that time, you will have to prove that you have done a substantial work."

"Thank you Reena. Fr. Bernard has told me that you will have to contact him only for all the money matters."

That night after her child slept, she opened the laptop and dialed Alok's number on Skype. He was very glad to see her after long.

When her beautiful face appeared on the screen, she said,

"Hey. How are you Alok?"

"I am good. I have sent the final version of my book. I think it may take a month. The final launch is going to be in Bangalore. You have to grace the occasion. You have to illuminate the hall by the radiant light emitted by your face."

"Stop it. I know, you are an English professor."

"Tell me, how is it in Udupi."

"Not good. I am successful, but am left with no time for myself. Sometimes, I feel as if I am wasting my time. As usual, Allan is confined to himself. George is alright. If I can get him married to the girl he likes, he will settle down to a good quality of life and a decent standard of living. I am worried about Joseph. So far, he has been revolting softly. I am afraid of the situation, what if he chooses the path of aggression? I was very much upset when I came to know about the bad deeds of my father. I want to meet my grandfather. I thought I will share all my feelings with you."

"You don't worry. You are a great healer. Your songs are soothing and so are your good words. You will overcome all these complex situations."

"We have to meet in Bangalore. I want to talk to you personally."

"What do you find interesting in me?"

"I enjoy talking to you. Your resonant voice is exciting.

It stimulates my nerves. I want explanations for some beautiful Kannada songs. We are preparing an album. I met a Kannada professor who has invited me to Bangalore. I will take his help in selecting the songs. I will ask him to give me the synopsis and a critical appreciation of the each song. I will analyze the emotions that can be conveyed through the song. When once you explain that, I can get into the mood of the song. This is more a professional relationship."

"Since, it is a professional assignment, you have to pay a fee," he said with a happy tone.

She was excited, "I am yours Alok. I am prepared to give you anything you ask."

Her voice was sexy, exciting and melodious more than ever. The hidden feelings in her mind had come out spontaneously in a soft husky form.

"Meet me at the airport tomorrow 9.30 pm,"she said.

Alok was thrilled with that voice and the naughty wink in her eye inviting him as if for a kiss or an embrace. She kissed his face on the screen. He returned it.

Alok was waiting at the airport. This time he was more eager and seemed to be restless. He waved his hand as soon as he saw her. She was draped in a simple new cotton saree. She looked very graceful. She was carrying the child in her arms. She said,

"Hey. It is nice to see you after such a long time."

"It is my pleasure Revathi". He held her hands in his hands and gently pressed them. Revathi experienced a current running through her body.

"It is very cold here. Stand here. I will bring the car."

"Revathi covered the child with a small blanket. Alok came near the place where she was waiting. He loaded her suitcases into the car.

As they were travelling along, "These three months, I would have to stay in Bangalore. I don't know what Vasundhara thinks about this trip. She is excited at the prospect of having the baby under her care for a longer time," Revathi wondered.

"So, what is your program?" Alok asked her.

"I will be recording a few songs. There is one programme in the City Institute. That is a major event. I have a couple of musical concerts. But, the most important part of this programme is my plan of producing a CD of devotional songs and romantic songs of the Navodaya period. This idea was mooted by the Kannada professor, whom I met in Chennai. He was very much attracted by my voice. He told me that he would have a small get-together at his house where some distinguished Kannada and English professors and music lovers would meet. I am going to do this for my pleasure. It is not a commercial venture. It is just an act of gratitude for the old couple, who travelled all the way to Chennai, just to attend my concert. This programme is a sort of curtain riser for my plan. The professor told me the sad story of his daughter-in-law, who lost her husband recently in a road accident. She is now pregnant. He told me that my song in YouTube made her relieve her emotional stress. She keeps listening to my alaaps even while she is driving on her way to the office."

"That is great Revathi. You have donned the role of a healer. As a nurse you used to heal the body pains of your patients. Now, you have proved that you can heal their minds as well."

"I think we have approached our destination." Vasundhara was waiting near the door to receive them.

"Welcome back Revathi."

"Hi Vasundhara". She embraced her into a warm hug.

"How is Ananya, my precious baby?"

"She is fine. Over to you now."

"I will take this job most willingly." She took the child in her arms. She kissed the child on the cheeks, forehead and the palms of hands on the feet.

"Let us have dinner. It is hot and simple. Nothing fancy." Vasundhara invited Revathi in.

They talked more than they ate. Alok ate as fast as he could and went to his bedroom. The two ladies ate very slowly with Revathi telling her entire story.

"How could he be so cruel?" Vasundhara was telling Revathi.

"My next task is to find my father wherever he is. I will make him come and accept his mistake. I want him accept Mary as his daughter and conduct the marriage."

"Is it impossible? Men of that kind never change. It was your mother's mistake to love him and run away with such a wicked person. Eventually, she paid the price by her death."

Then they went to their respective bedrooms. The next morning Revathi left for her recording.

She was welcomed as a big star. The musicians felt very happy that a singer of Revathi's caliber had given consent to sing a Kannada song. The music director, Ravindra looked like a young college student. But, the way he conducted the whole thing convinced Revathi that he had an in-depth knowledge of music. He explained to Revathi the pattern.

"Madam, I am obsessed with your alaaps. So, I have decided to have an alaap in every song in this film. In the background score, I have planned to have there are lots of alaaps. I have planned. Most of them will be in Malkauns. Since this is a novel-based film, with a strong story line we wanted you very much for this film. We knew that you were extremely busy in Chennai. It is our good fortune that we could secure some dates".

Another young and smart looking gentleman came and introduced himself.

"I am Ramesh Chandra. I am the director of this film. Since this film is based on a popular novel, expectations are very high. The alaaps play a very important role. They run throughout the film. Virtually, the heroine's feelings are conveyed through these alaaps. The story is about a married woman who is attracted by a young theater artist. She keeps meeting him frequently and her mind is oscillating between the extremities of her family responsibilities and the strong force of attraction of love and lust. We have made some changes in the story with the permission of the author. Emotions play the lead role. Spoken words are relatively less. I think you have a greater job than the heroine."

"I will do my best Ramesh Sir. I don't feel like calling you Sir. Can I call you Ramesh?"

"I consider that a favour madam."

"You can call me Revathi. I don't want to be called Madam. That puts me at a distance."

The entire team was astonished at Revathi's simplicity. They knew she had won the hearts of the Tamil people. She had won the National award for her very first song.

When she sat and closed her eyes and started the first alaap there was silence and every one held their breath and seemed to wonder if it was actually possible to sing like that!

The director Ramesh Chandra was very happy with Revathi's alaap.

"I think I have captured the mood of the heroine. I know how to explain the situation. This alaap will put the heroine automatically into the groove of the story line. Revathi, thank you for such a wonderful alaap."

The music director Ravindra respectfully acknowledged Revathi's singing.

"This was a great experience for me which I will cherish for a very long time. It was indeed a great learning experience. You were the master of the situation. There was very little improvisation I could think of. The Yemen Kalyani composition, my God! That was a treat. I never imagined that my compositions could be so divine, melodious. I don't know what to say." He was in tears.

Revathi replied,"My mother died as soon as I was born. Somehow, I had those feelings. When the situation was explained to me about the heroine's helplessness and uncertainty about her future without knowing what to do, whether to go back to her family or join her lover, I was thinking about my mother. She too had to face such a complex situation in her life. I think I became emotional in singing. That is why I took the Yaman alaap."

"The hindola is your forte. That song is charged with melody. We are using the alaaps in our teaser extensively and highlight it." Ramesh Chandra replied.

"I could enjoy every word, every syllable. I knew the meaning of the words. The mood was created spontaneously and the words flowed in resonance with the tune. I must thank the great musicians".

Within ten days, she had completed her songs and the alaaps.

She took leave from them after the recording for the day was over. When she was travelling in the car towards home, the cell phone bell rang.

"I am Dr. Rao from Mysore university. Do you remember me? I met you in Chennai. We had come to Chennai just to attend tour concert. This Saturday we want you to come to our house. My daughter-in-law is excited at the prospect of meeting you."

"Please text me your address Sir. I will come on Saturday."

"Oh! No. I am coming to pick you up. I was told that you stay in Jayanagar. That is very close to my house."

"I am in Jayanagar third block. Please come near the swimming pool and give me a call."

Revathi briefed Vasundhara about this meeting. "It

is really sad to know about that girl. I think your presence can make her feel happy, you should do it."

Prof. Rao located the address very easily.

They went to an old bungalow. He ~~lead~~ led her inside the house.

"Rashmi, please see who has come to meet you. Your favourite singer Revathi has come."

Rashmi was dressed in a nice white silk saree.

She said, "You have a very beautiful face. You look prettier than what I saw on YouTube. Our generation had forgotten the immortal Kannada song, "Chandramukhi Praanasakhi". You made all of us sing. Your song in praise of the womanhood made all women proud of ourselves. I am a big fan of yours. I have fallen in love with your voice." Rashmi could not control her excitement.

"That Tamil song, my God! What a song? The alaap you have given to it initially is something unimaginable. No wonder, that song won you the National award. It is very nice of you madam to come here. I never expected that gesture."

"When Dr. Rao was waiting to meet me as I got down from the dais, I felt a sense of awe. I sat with him and listened to your sad story, I decided I should meet you. When I see such music lovers, I feel that I have achieved something in my life. When he told me that you keep playing that song while driving to your office, I felt like coming at that moment itself and give you a hug." Revathi also seemed to be getting emotional by Rashmi's excitement.

"The way that speaker spoke, his voice was so captivating! He looks similar to our English lecturer in our college. How did he get involved in your programme?"

"The whole programme was his concept. He liked my voice very much. I am actually a nurse by profession. I was helping his father-in-law in Udupi for post- operative treatment. That is where I met Alok."

"Yeah. I remember now. Aloknath Vyasathirtha. The girls were crazy about his voice. Some science students used to cut other classes and attend his poetry classes. He was known for reciting poetry lines very beautifully. I was told that he married his own student."

"True."

"You are indeed very lucky. You have a beautiful face, a melodious voice and everything a woman can dream of."

"But, you should listen to my story. I am Revathi Allan. I lost my mother the next instant I was born. I grew up in a boarding run by our church in Udupi. I fell in love with a cab driver who used to come to the church for assisting the parish priest. I gave birth to a boy.

He was with us only five years. While playing at the beach, the sea waves carried him to deep waters. He did not return……."

"Your story is also very sad," Rashmi said.

"I was in a state of mental trauma. My mentor Dr. Kalyani helped me to come out of depression. Alok encouraged me to sing. He brought me to that college function. That is where I started my journey," Revathi narrated her story.

"What about you? Losing husband at such a young age is very tragic. Don't you think of a second marriage?"

"My father-in-law and mother-in- law tried their best to convince me to marry again. I didn't like the idea. I thought of performing my husband's duty by remaining here. I was pregnant. I can never think of such things…"

Revathi admired Rashmi's sacrifice. She had not rejected life. She was prepared to sacrifice her future in the memory of her husband. The birth of a child may bring back light in her life.

"You have a girl child now?"

"It is not my husband's. It is Alok's child. We had an affair. I want to be honest with you. After a few more years, the gossamers of love will flow over your body. Instead of lamenting over your past, try to enjoy the future. Fall in love with someone, who can give you love. Make your ~~love~~ life more beautiful."

"I am sorry. May be I am very timid or old fashioned. I cannot take such a bold stand. I will remain the way I am. I do not find fault in your view. I am still not mature enough."

"Anyway, don't forget to call me up when you get such a thought."

"So,… I will take your leave. Before going, let me apologize to you for my unsolicited intervention in your personal life. If I have hurt you, I am very sorry."

"You don't have to feel sorry or apologize. You have proved that you are a great human being. I can look up to you as a good friend in some difficult moments.

"Once again, I am extremely grateful to you. You are so down to earth, that I forgot for a moment you are the celebrity singer, Revathi."

She came out into the drawing room where Dr. Rao and his wife were waiting.

"You seem to have chatted for a long time?" The couple waited with a smile and a humble look. "It was a heart-to-heart talk. I told her about my son's death. She told me about your son's death."

"Revathi, I have fixed a programme. Next month, on the tenth. It is a Sunday. The committee members were pleasantly shocked to know that I had met you and got your consent on our platform. They have agreed to pay whatever fee you fix."

"Sir. It is better I leave those things to you. There are two things here. One, this is a prestigious platform on which some very great singers have sung. Second, I wanted to express my gratitude to your gesture of coming all the way to attend my musical concert in Chennai. After coming here, I got a good friend like Rashmi," she replied with a lot of affection.

"Sir, I want a favour from you. You have to select some of the finest poems of the Navodaya period. I want to sing them in my own way and produce a CD. I also want a synopsis of those poems. And make it a literary and musical masterpiece."

"Thanks for your friendly talk with Rashmi. I will complete the project you have assigned to me as early as I can. I will call you when I complete this."

"Sir . You are very kind to me. I was very hesitant to ask you. But, I felt that I should request you."

"It is very nice of you. My wife has some small gift for you."

Mrs. Rao came with a silver plate in her hand. The plate contained some fruits and jasmine flowers and a bag containing a silk saree.

"Madam. What is this? Do I deserve all this? I came here for a chat. No madam, I will just take these flowers and fruits."

"Please don't say no. It is Rashmi's gift to you. This morning she went to the shop herself and bought this. You look like goddess Lakshmi. We never expected that a great artist like you would come to our house."

Revathi accepted the gift in all humility and prostrated to the elderly couple.

She came back to the house and narrated all the incidents to Vasundhara.

"We people from Mysore still have that tradition of honouring artists."

"I really feel sad about that girl. She is an engineer and refused to accept the idea of a remarriage."

"You shouldn't have suggested that."

"I apologized to her. But, she said that even her father-in-law and mother-in- law offered to find a boy for her."

"That girl has a good samskaara."

"The modern woman has to be bold. She has to come out from her shell."

"You and Alok share~~d~~ a platform and ~~gave~~ give a beautiful lecture on this. It will be wonderful to hear. But, ~~I~~ in many cases it is not practical."

"I like the way, you made fun of us," Alok said.

"Thanks for the like. Revathi, take your child. She is crying."

"Thank you Vasundhara for taking care of the child.

"This time you must thank Alok. He had been holding the child in his arms throughout this evening."

"Thank you Alok," she said smilingly in a husky voice and looked at him radiating light from her bright face."

Vasundhara went out to fetch some groceries along with her children.

Revathi started speaking to Alok.

"I met Dr. Rao, the Kannada professor that I had spoken to you about. He will give us a list of poems and a brief synopsis of all the poems. I will set the tune with the help of musicians and will be singing them.

You have to give a brief introduction to those songs in your voice. I may get the poems and the notes within a week."

"I have agreed to do this project. But we have not talked about the professional charges."

" What professional charges?" Revathi asked.

" I want you. I love you Revathi. I want to spend time with you. We are not getting any time to stay alone. Just the two of us. We have to sit and talk."

"That cannot happen hereafter. We are bound by some moral values," Revathi replied.

"It was at your instance that we stayed in the hotel that night. You just wanted a child. You manipulated and exploited me. Now you are talking of moral values," Alok retaliated.

"I had a good reason. I wanted motherhood. I didn't hide anything. I told everyone. Nobody found fault with us. Fr. Bernard, Sr. Clara, everyone supported me. Vasundhara also saw a reason in my actions. She took it in a very magnanimous manner. If now we indulge in sex, it is going to be a crime. I will be meeting you just to satisfy our sensuous needs."

"Let it be like that. Your husky voice kills me. It instills in me a sexual urge which you alone can satisfy me. I cannot think of infidelity or any fear of lying. I will tell Vasundhara that I have an irresistible temptation which I cannot overcome. I want you Revathi. I just cannot stop thinking of your beautiful body," Alok said without hiding his feelings any longer.

"Alok, the whole world is watching the release of your book. You told me that you have given a beautiful end. Is this the end you had planned?" Revathi asked.

"That is fiction. The writer has the liberty to make anything happen,." Alok tried to defend himself.

Revathi replied, "But this is life. God has authored our roles. We can play just that. Today, I met that young girl. She is a smart beautiful girl. She is educated. In the prime of her youth, she lost her husband. Her husband's parents are willing to find her a boy and get her married. But she wants to remain with them and wishes to serve them till the end. After seven years of marriage, after losing my son, I entered into a relation with you. I became pregnant with your child. I know that you are Vasundhara's husband. In spite of that I continue to love you. I was not taking revenge against my husband. I wanted to have the joy of motherhood. Vasundhara taught me the quality of mercy. Mercy is twice blessed. It blesses the one who gives it and who takes it.

Meeting with Rashmi gave me a different dimension to my life. She taught me the importance of loyalty to love in life.

When you were having that complex psychic disorder, I had prayed in churches. I went to temples. I went to Mantralaya. All these things increased my inner strength. I became a strong person.

Infact, when you asked me for your professional fee on the phone, I was excited at the prospect of restarting our affair. But, today after I met that girl, I understood the importance of restraint in the quality of our mind.

You are a highly respected teacher. Students look up to you with awe. You have to manifest yourself with dignity and evoke a sense of respect. We are free to do anything in life now. Tonight, we can go and have sex . It is not a big problem. But the greatness lies in our restraint, our ability to control our thoughts and actions. Alok, I still love you. But, pure love is devoid of all sensuous feelings. It is a mutual respect for each other. It is a mutual submission, surrender."

Alok sat speechless. He just started admiring her in his mind.

'Thank God. I was about to commit another sin. If that had happened really, Vasundhara would never have excused me. My sons are important to me. My family is important to me. I will not cheat on Vasundhara.,' Hhe said to himself.

"Revathi, thank you for opening my eyes. You made me realize the importance of values of our system in which marriage is an important institution. As you said, we will maintain our friendly relation. We will keep it in its purest form, chaste, simple, but adorable."

"By the way, who asked you to go to Mantralaya?" Alok asked her.

"You were very sick. You had such a complex mental disorder which could have driven you to dementia or some nervous disorder. I was shattered. Immediately, I made a confession of all that happened to Vasundhara. I told the doctor so that they get the case history correctly. I made a true confession of everything to Vasundhara.

Vasundhara told me, that when you lost your mother, you were about to enter a similar level of depression. Vasundhara took you to Mantralaya. She told me that she introduced you to the performance of 'Urulu Seva' i.e. rolling around the temple corridor in wet clothes after bathing in the river. She told me that you had no belief in all this. You only believe in karmayoga. But at that time, without uttering a word you quietly followed her and performed the Seva. It was out of sheer love for your mother that you carried out that task. Vasundhara then took me to the Pooja room and showed me your mother's photo. She then requested me to go to Mantralaya and meditate. Because I was pregnant at that time, I could not obviously perform the Urulu Seva. And if I did not even want to go to Mantralaya, I must take up some vow which was permitted in my religion. But for you, I agreed to visit Mantralaya and have vowed to take you and our child also some day;" she said.

"That was it Alok. Vasundhara was observing all the religious vows so perfectly that it appeared as if she was performing a penance. I was trying to emulate her. I was fasting once in a week. I think our prayers were answered.

Now tell me. Was I selfish? Did I manipulate you? Did I exploit the situation I created?'

Alok said after a pause, "I am terribly sorry. I apologize. I want to repeat my favourite line.

Nobility thy name is woman."

With the cloud of misunderstanding having been cleared, Revathi and Alok decided to start their new venture.

Revathi completed all her projects and went towards Udupi. Alok maintained a strict professional relation with Revathi.

They produced three audio CDs. They were released in the market. All the audio CDs were a big success. The reviews were good.

Dr. Rao spoke to Revathi and congratulated Revathi. He said he was delighted to listen to the popular devara naamaas. He particularly liked the explanations given initially for each song.

He said, "Who is that speaker? Apart from the brief notes I had given, he has explained the importance of the usage of the words. I would like to meet that gentleman."

Revathi replied, "I will certainly bring him Sir."

She requested Alok to accompany her to meet Dr. Rao."

Dr. Rao was extremely happy to meet Alok. He welcomed him very warmly.

"Revathi is a great singer. Her songs are soulful and divine. But your explanations and commentaries are superb. The way you have given the brief history of Kannada literature and the emergence of the Navodaya movement is a marvel. My notes were very brief. But, you have enriched it with your comments. I liked the way you brought a parallelism between the romantic period in English poetry and the Navodaya movement in Kannada poetry. Your observation that there was a profound impact of the romantic poets on some of our very great poets in Kannada may land you in some controversy in the Kannada literary circles"

"Yes. I agree with you Sir. I want it to be both evocative and provocative. Even if it is just provocative, I will be happy."

"Your knowledge in Kannada poetry seems to be remarkable. A professor of English talking Kannada so clearly and in such a voice was an excellent prelude to the songs that followed."

"Thank you Sir. I feel honoured to get such beautiful appreciation from a learned professor like you."

"Revathi told me that you have written a novel." '

"Yes Ssir. The title of the novel is Hindola. I have written about the emotional journey that a woman undergoes in our social framework. The hindola raaga is used as a symbol. As the raaga oscillates between the extreme emotions of agony and ecstacy, the musical waves play as an undercurrent throughout the novel.

It is going to be published next month. I request you to grace the occasion and give your blessings. I request you to read it and give your critical review.

"Certainly. It will be my pleasure."

Revathi had brought fruits and flowers. She placed in a silver plate and offered that to him.

Dr. Rao took the small envelope and asked ,

"What is this Revathi?"

"It is a token of my gratitude. It is a cheque. It is a very small amount."

"Alright. It is actually a big amount. I am not going to refuse it. But I am donating it to our association. We are giving some merit scholarships for the poor students. I will be giving it in your name."

"I am honoured."

They took leave of Dr. Rao. Rashmi just entered the house. She had finished her office work. She was excited to see Revathi and Alok.

"Sir. I am an old student of your college. I studied English just for one year. You were taking only degree classes for English major students. I remember your poetry classes were very famous. Daddy spoke very highly about your explanations for the songs rendered by Revathi."

Alok thanked her.

They were back at home.

Revathi was all in awe and admiration for Alok's knowledge. She thought that it was her good fortune to be his friend. She thought and said to herself.

'If such a great man wants her as his lover, there is nothing wrong to surrender herself both bodily and mentally.'

But Vasundhara's affection, the way she was trying to help her and treating her as if she is her own sister made her to forget about these lustful desires.

Her renewed faith in the ultimate supremacy of human values seemed to have elevated her maturity in thought and actions.

Chapter Fourteen

* * *

Joseph was waiting for her at the airport. He saw Revathi carrying her child. Revathi was surprised to see Joseph coming to pick her up. He booked a cab. He very lovingly offered to carry the child.

They moved together towards Udupi.

"How are you Joseph?" She asked.

"I am fine. You cautioned me at the right time. My friend who approached me to sell the land turned out to be a fraud. All his transactions and business proposals seemed to be illegal and bogus. Thank God. I was very angry when you discouraged me. But now, things have proved that you are right. I will henceforth take your advice seriously. I am doing my computer courses. I am finding them very interesting. I think that we have to set up from small beginnings and grow. I will work very hard and try to achieve something.

"It is so nice to hear such good things from you. I have two important tasks. First, George's marriage and second yours."

They reached Udupi in an hour's time.

Revathi:

After my Bangalore trip, I observed that there was a change in Joseph's attitude. He appeared to be very responsible.

He had finished a few courses in computers. His typing speed increased and his graphic skills were also enhanced. He was very much interested in photography. He wanted to start a press in Bangalore. We had a meeting with Fr. Bernard. Fr. Bernard agreed to our proposal.

I could meet Sr. Clara that day. She was very happy on seeing the child.

We first decided to build a shed to house the printing machinery. Joseph set up a small office. The money I had earned in the recordings in Chennai and Bangalore, was not sufficient for this type of investment. We took a loan from the bank. We could get fifty lakhs as we had our land as security. Allan had come to sign the agreement. He cautioned me about the business.

"Be careful. Joseph's friends are not good."

I told him, "He has changed a lot. He said that he did not want to drive cabs and was interested in computer work. I asked him to join some computer courses. He has completed a few courses. Let us hope for the best. I will not involve him in any financial dealings. I will make him work.

Let us see… how it works?"

We decided to have a technical expert to run the whole press. We inserted an advertisement. We were able to find Sunil Rego, who was willing to work at the salary we offered.

He seemed to know the work that had to be done. He made a layout plan. We were able to buy the latest printing machinery. The installation work was completed.

All the three brothers were united now. Each one was trying to help the other. I consulted a lawyer. He helped us in registering the company as a publishing house. All of them agreed to my proposal that it should be named as Grace Publishing and Printing House. Sunil Rego was appointed as the senior manager.

We were searching for clients. Fr. Bernard helped us in providing some business links. I approached Krishna. He helped me in providing some contracts.

We started our work with all sincerity. We worked hard. We got orders for printing text books, fiction, and religious works.

Joseph worked very hard. He was occupied with work and worked like a demon. Sunil was a great guide.

Alok had called me.

"Hey. It is me Alok. My book is being launched by my publishers. You had promised to attend. You will be singing a beautiful Hindola song. Next Monday... Please come here on Sunday. Can I invite Allan?"

"Sure. I will ask him to come. I will try to bring his brothers also."

"We will meet in Bangalore next Monday."

I was making arrangements for George's marriage. George was always behind me helping me to carry the child and assist me. Allan was also there with us and helped us.

We performed the marriage on a grand scale.

With George's marriage getting over, I had finished my task partially. Joseph had to settle down in his business and finally in his life.

I had another important task. I had to discover my origins. I had the address of my grandfather. I thought of tracing him first. I looked at the address. It was a village near Kanyakumari. It was a village very close to the Kerala border. I decided to travel to Trivandrum by flight. I booked two air tickets to Trivandrum. I booked a cab on line to pick me and take me to Marthandam. I decided to take help from the local people to locate the village and finally reached my grandfather.

I entered the village. The cab could manage to pass through the narrow streets of the village. I stopped at a place when I located it. Four people had gathered at a place. They were holding a Tamil news paper and discussing some local politics.

I approached them and asked,

"I have this address. Can you please tell me where

this house is?"

They pointed at a narrow lane.

I could reach my grandfather's house. I saw him seated in a cane chair.

I presumed that he was my grandfather. I asked him,

"Are you Varadaraja Sir?"

Yes. Who are you?'

I took out the photo from my bag and showed it to him.

He went inside and brought his spectacles.

Wearing his spectacles he was able to make out that they were indeed his own daughters. He said, "They are my daughters Valli and Eshwari. Who are you? Where did you get this photo?"

"I am Valli's daughter. I was deserted by you. You left me in the church and went away. I met your brother, Chinnappan. He gave me your address….

I have come to meet my father. I want to talk to him."

"I am delighted to see you child. You have grown very beautifully. You look like your mother. Come on. Please be seated. I have nothing to offer you….

I will try to get you some fruits atleast."

"Don't bother. I have brought some fruits for you. Please have it."

I placed the fruit basket.

Tears were flowing down Varadaraja's eyes. "He came like a demon and destroyed our family. We lost both our daughters."

"Thatha….Can I ask you one thing.

…. Is my father alive?"

"I really don't know. He had come here once, a few months ago. He was talking very incoherently. He shouted at me and asked,

'Where is Valli? Who killed her? Where is my daughter? I want her back?"

"He was not drunk. He was shouting and screaming.

Then he went away."

"Where do you think I can find him?"

"There is a small coffee shop near the bus stand. I have found Velu often sitting there and chatting with that Govinda, the owner of that shop."

I went to the bus stand. I located the coffee shop.

I asked , "Who is Govinda?"

"It is me. What do you want Madam?"

"I am Varadaraja's granddaughter. Velu is my father. Can you please tell me something about him? Chinnappan thatha told me that you will know his whereabouts."

"He keeps roaming around. He was a good actor. Now he has lost his balance. We can't understand what he is trying to say. Many mistake him to be a beggar. The village children are amused by his strange actions and words. They chase him and try pelting stones at him. When I see that, I bring him. I calm him down. He sleeps here for some time and goes away. He may come any time now. When he feels hungry, he comes here."

"Why are you treating him so kindly."

"In his good days, he used to earn. When I set up this hotel, he had helped me with a loan of five hundred rupees. I had not repaid that loan. He has forgotten those things. Whenever he comes here dejected, I give him some food and ask him to sleep.

He takes his food. He sleeps on this bench and sings for some time. He disappears all of a sudden."

"When will he come here again?"

"I don't know. But, he will certainly come."

"How to meet him? I must see him."

"You stay here for a day or two. There is a lodge in Marthandam. You give me your phone number. When he comes here, I will call you."

"That would be fine. I will go to my grandfather's house."

I thought of staying with my grandfather. I wanted to

collect some more information about my father.

I went to my grandfather's house. He was sitting on his cane chair.

"Did you find Govinda?"

"Yes thatha. He asked me to stay here for a couple of days."

"Where will you stay? Is it possible for you? A small crowd had gathered near my house. When I asked them why they had gathered there, they told me that you are a great singer and you sing in films. How can you stay in this hut?"

"Never mind. The pleasure of talking to you and to assist you is all I need."

"I don't have anything to offer. Please go to Marthandam. There is one hotel where you can have some good food."

Revathi gave five hundred rupees to her driver and asked him to fetch some fruits, bread.

"See whether you can get some milk."

After two days Revathi received a phone call.

"Madam, it is me Govinda speaking. Velu has come. It looks as if he has fallen somewhere. There was some bleeding near the temple of his head. I took a wet cloth and tried to stop the bleeding. I have tied a wet cloth on the wound. The bleeding has stopped and now he is sleeping. You can come here and talk to him when he is awake."

Revathi rushed towards the small hotel.

She saw her father sleeping. Govinda said,

"He is my cousin. His mother took care of me when I was a child. I want him to stop this habit of roaming around in streets like a mad man. It is very disheartening to see people throwing stones at him and provoking him."

"Yes uncle. I know that he has harassed our family very badly. When I came here, I was so much upset that I felt like killing him, even if it meant going to the jail. But, he is my father. All these days I did not know, whether he was dead or alive. After seeing these things, I cannot just desert him. I think I will take him to some hospital now. He is in a state of delirium. He has to be taken to a doctor. I have to transport him to Bangalore. He has to be admitted to Nimhans. I will try to get the best treatment."

Uncle can you come to Bangalore along with me? It is very difficult for me to take him to Bangalore. I have to take care of this child also."

Govinda said, "I will accompany you".

They went straight to a nursing home in Marthandam. The doctor took a CT scan of the brain. The doctor after a thorough examination said, "You will have to take him to Nimhans in Bangalore. His condition is very critical."

Revathi booked a flight at the earliest available time. Fortunately, she could get a flight that night. She brought her father to Bangalore.

She called for a private ambulance. The ambulance arrived within fifteen minutes.

They quickly transported him to Nimhans. Revathi managed to admit him to the emergency ward.

Velu was put on glucose.

"The scan shows that he has a blood clot in the brain. He cannot be operated considering his present physical condition. He has neglected his health completely. There is a partial failure of the nervous system. We will watch and see. He may be paralyzed. Another thing that can happen is that he may develop pneumonia. We will do our best."

Revathi was praying and said to herself.

"Let him die peacefully instead of suffering. I went in search of him to express my uncontrolled anger. In that fit of anger, I thought I would shoot him. But now, I am looking after him as a dutiful daughter."

Three days later Velu died without even having a glimpse of mine.

My grandfather offered to perform the last rites.

There were conflicting emotions in my mind. This is the man who cheated my mother and deserted me. I was in search of this man and finally found him in his deathbed. Was my struggle worth all this?

That was the end of my journey of the discovery my origins. I was sobbing uncontrollably. I was wrecked emotionally.

Fr. Bernard made a valiant effort to console me. Sr. Clara was carrying the child. Allan came to know of my sad situation into which I had gotten myself. George and Joseph were there. Alok was looking at me very sadly.

Govinda said. I will do the last rites. He is my cousin after all.

"Govinda uncle, I will perform all his rites. Please make all the arrangements for the cremation. I can leave this place with a sense of fulfillment.

The feelings of anger that were burning in her mind turned into cold waves of compassion".

A priest of Velu's community was arguing with the other priests about the issue of letting a Christian girl to perform the last rites.

Govinda was convincing them.

"That lady is a celebrity. If you try to create any problem, it is going to be a big issue. People from the press and TV will come. Then some other priest will come and take all the money. Be wise enough to conduct this and take whatever she can offer you,"

Govinda's talk seemed to convince them.

I went through the whole process religiously. I had told them not to miss a single step in the entire procedure. The seven or eight ablutions did not appear to cool my body and mind.

After performing all the ablutions, I sat down in one corner. It appeared as if my emotional journey in finding the roots of my family has terminated. I had stood heavy hearted at the cross roads.

Allan came near me and said, " Let us go to our house in Goa. You as a mentor have done a tremendous job. Take some time for you. You have sacrificed very much for our family.

George is married. Joseph is looking after the publishing house. He has become matured and talks like a business professional. Both are well settled."

I thought that Allan was correct. His tone was genuine and honest. I found my father. I have tried to serve him in his last days. I have performed his last rites. It is time for me to go away from the innermost core of emotional content lying deep within my mind. I was feeling week within. But I had a deep sense of relief.

John came near me,

" The publishing house is doing very well. Tomorrow I have an appointment with an executive in a software firm. I will finish my work and join you in Udupi after two days."

We reached Udupi late at night. Allan said, "You can stay here as long as you wish. But please think of me as a good friend and do not hesitate to approach me for any kind of help."

I was moving on. Time was rolling.

It was about three months. In these three months I had answered hundreds of phone calls from various friends, including some reputed actors, actresses, music directors, producers, directors and others. I was moved by their kind words.

Shankar Vasishta spoke to me and said, "This is a phase which every individual has to pass through. Please do not keep lamenting over the inevitable incident. Keep on moving. The best way to get over this phase of sorrow is to get involved in your professional work. Start signing the contracts, recordings and your routine"

"Yes Shankar. I think that is a good advice. Thank you."

I started my normal work. I was travelling a lot in those days. In Bangalore, Vasundhara was a big source of help to me. She used to take care of my daughter. I could go to Chennai leaving my daughter in her loving hands.

Alok drove me once to my recording studio. He offered to take me to the studio every day.

One day as he was driving Revathi to the studio, he said, "My book is getting launched this Sunday. The publishers are promoting the book in a grand manner. Without taking your consent, I have taken the liberty to include your programme. You will have to sing all our favorite compositions. Dr. Rao, will be the chief guest. He read through the whole book and has written a nice foreword. He will speak about the book. The book will be released by my teacher Mangala. This was a suggestion given to me by Ramaswamy, my classmate in the school. He is a very famous reviewer and a columnist in leading newspapers."

"That is great. Alok you have done it," Revathi spoke very happily.

"I am indebted to you. You are the real inspiration for this book,"Alok replied.

"I have read it when it was half completed. I am curious to know how you have ended it," Revathi seemed curious to know the end.

"So... how are your recordings going on ?" Alok said trying to change the topic.

"Umm. ...Fine".

They reached the recording studio. Alok bade her good bye and went to the college.

Revathi had to sing a sad song that day. The director was explaining to her the situation.

"The heroine is a widow. She has lost her father and she is trying to overcome her grief. We are using the backdrop of the sea, the sea waves, the blue sky, the mountainous range, the green nature. The song itself is a lyrical beauty. I particularly wanted you to sing this. I am sure this will be a visual treat and your voice will add grandeur to it. We want your Malkauns alaaps in between. The alaaps will be used throughout the film."

Revathi's mood synchronized with the song. She was totally involved in the song and sang as if she was the heroine. When she was singing the alaaps, the painful feelings in her heart melted and flowed. All the musicians had tears in their eyes.

The young heroine Bhavana, who was known for her sensitive acting, had come just to listen to Revathi. She had closed her eyes. When the recording was complete, she came to Revathi and gave her a warm hug.

"I have heard your songs. This is the first time I have seen you recording live. I understood the mood of the situation in the song. I am mentally prepared. I will be doing my best. But the song will steal the show. You are a great singer. It is my good luck that you are singing this beautiful song."

"Bhavana, you have those beautiful eyes. Are you a dancer."

"Not really. But I can display some of the dance movements gracefully. I would love to play roles that portray the complex feelings in the helpless situations a woman faces. I consider that a challenge and I get empathetically involved in such situations."

Bhavana continued, "I had listened to your songs. But, seeing you singing live is a wonderful experience. The way you feel the song and give expressions is something beyond our imagination. This is a new learning experience for me. I will try to give the best of my thoughts and feelings to this role"

Revathi was delighted that an actress of Bhavana's caliber came to her and talked to her.

Joseph called up Revathi. He had asked her to stay back in Bangalore. He was speaking over the cell phone, "I am meeting a very important client. We will go together in the evening."

Revathi got some free time. She entered into Alok's time. Alok had kept a few pages of his book in his room. She started reading those pages. She was about to start reading that. Alok entered the room unexpectedly inside. He said,

"Don't read them now. I will speak about it on the launching day."

"Sorry. I shouldn't have intruded into your room."

"Never mind ...Have you practiced your songs?"

" You shouldn't know it," Revathi said in a teasing manner.

" Please do not mistake me. Those pages are the ending part, I had planned ~~it~~ earlier. Now the end is different. The book is already printed with the new end."

"Alright. Wish you all the best."

"I am a little tensed. I have invested a good amount of my earnings into publishing this book. If it is appreciated by the public, I have won the war. Otherwise, there is a need for concern."

"Have you got it reviewed?"

"Let the book come out. I will give it to some well known critics. Let us see. Ultimately, it depends on the story and the strength of the story to attract the reader."

"You will be successful. Don't worry," Revathi said while encouraging him.

Chapter Fifteen

* * *

Revathi:

Joseph had come to pick me. I introduced him to Alok. They shook hands. They didn't have any area of common interest. But, Joseph was smart and talked to Alok very happily.

We took leave of them and started moving towards Udupi. He started talking slowly,

"Allan is very hesitant to talk to us after Gracey's death. He has not come here even once. I went to Goa to invite him to see the new building we have built. He congratulated me and wished me well. He is trying to hide something away from all of us. I thought that he was upset about the division of property. George and I thought about it. We thought that we will again sit together and make redistribution. When I went to his house, I saw a young beautiful girl. She was preparing to go to the college. Allan was giving some medicine to the old watchman. The girl is the watchman's daughter.

"He was not willing to talk to me. He said the property distribution is a closed chapter. If you do not have anything to talk, I must leave. I told him that I was changed now and that we all wanted him to live with you and your daughter. But, he absolutely have me a stern reply of not returning.

I was so desperate to know what was going on, that I followed that girl. I asked her who she was and how was Allan related to him. She told me that Allan was her protector and he was her elder brother. I told her that we all thought he had married a Goan girl. But, she refused and defended him saying that he was very particular of his moral values. He would never marry or stay with any other girl." He informed everything to Revathi.

" Reena. I want to tell you one thing.

Today I attended a one-day programme for updating our software technology for our publication work. A lady had come to give a talk. She looked like a pregnant woman.

She conducted the programme very well. I helped her in setting up her laptop, the projector and the screen. She is very smart and appears to be very intelligent. I want to marry a girl like that."

"Did you talk to her?"

"She thanked me and asked me what I was doing. I told her that I wanted to update the software for my printing."

She asked me if I was from Udupi.

I said, " Yes. Madam, what about you?

"I am from Mysore," she replied.

"I am glad she inspired you. Don't get motivated to love and marry someone. On the other hand, try to dream more about your ambitious projects. Some women entrepreneurs are very successful," Revathi warned him.

I was really inspired. A pregnant lady doing her duty in such a systematic manner ....Really! I felt that it was remarkable," Joseph spoke in awe.

"That is the greatness of a woman. She is a fighter. Let her story of hard work inspire you. What is her name?"

"I think, Rashmi or Lakshmi ... something like that."

"How is she?"

"I told you. Smart and intelligent."

"Is she beautiful?"

"She has a good appearance. She is not very fair. But there is a bright glow in her eyes.

We took a selfie. The one in the white saree is her," Joseph showed her the picture.

"That is Rashmi. I know her. I had been to her house. She is pregnant."

Revathi did not proceed to say anything about her. She thought that Rashmi was a strong woman and felt proud about her."

"I met her personally. I told you about."

Joseph had made a new office room. She saw a beautiful cabin with all facilities. It was air-conditioned with WiFi facility. The executive chair was vey posh. The walls of the room were paneled. The floor was carpeted. Joseph said,

"That is your office. The Chairman's house," Joseph said.

"Joseph , You work here. That small room is adequate for me."

"Reena, You should be here. Your very presence will be an inspiration."

Revathi was moved by Joseph's gestures. She called up Allan and apprised him of everything.

He said, "I wish I had that opportunity to work with you."

How is Alice?"

"She has done her exams well. She finished her CET exams. She is feeling bored to stay at home."

"Send her here. Let her assist me. She has basic knowledge of Computers… Right?"

"I don't know anything. I bought her a laptop. She keeps doing something with that. Yeah! I will send her to your place."

Alice went to their office. She was thrilled with the atmosphere. They set up a table for her. Initially Revathi just asked her to do some data entry work.

"She is really good. She is a very fast learner," Joseph remarked.

The CET exam results were out. Alice had secured a rank within thousand.

Allan had come to pick her up. They moved to Mangalore.

Alice secured a seat to study in the Manipal Engineering College. She got admitted. Revathi suggested that she could stay at home. Allan wanted her to stay in the hostel.

Alice started her four-year journey in Manipal hostel.

Alice used to visit us every Sunday. She used to be very friendly with Ananya. Their house used to be filled with life on Sundays.

Allan informed of the sad demise of his father's death. Revathi found it difficult to control him. But Allan proved that he is a great brother, yet again.

Revathi:

"Tomorrow we will have to leave for Bangalore. Alok's book is being released." I said.

All the brothers seemed to be busy with their own preoccupations. Nobody evinced interest in coming to the function.

I packed off to Mangalore. Allan droped me at the airport.

When I arrived in Bangalore, Alok was waiting for me at the airport.

He helped me in carrying the luggage.

Vasundhara was waiting near the entrance of her house. She was delighted to see Ananya. Ananya could walk slowly step-by-step. Vasundhara asked me,

"How are you Revathi?"

"It has been a long time since I saw you last. Please do come in."

It was an emotional moment for them.

When Revathi got a chance to talk to Alok, she asked him.

"What is the end?"

"Now you can read it. The book is going to be released this evening. You can read it tonight."

Revathi said,

"I am really curious to know the end. I am excited."

They went in the evening to a convention hall. The publishers had arranged a nice event. There was a good and sizeable audience. The general manager of the company Mr. Pai received Alok very warmly.

The function started with a recorded version of a prayer song of the company.

Mr. Pai welcomed the gathering. He started,

"It is our pleasure to have Dr. Ramachadra Rao amidst us. He is a scholar in English, Kannada and Samskruta. Some of the well known novels published by us were first reviewed by him. We are very grateful to you Sir for having reviewed this book and given your approval for publication. We extend a very warm welcome to you sir.

Aloknath Vyasathirtha, the author of this novel, presented the first few pages of this novel. To be honest, I did not know him. Out of curiosity, I went through the first few pages and I found it very interesting. I asked him to send the complete novel. He had discussions with our editorial team and finally we have brought out this book. I am very confident that this will be accepted by booklovers all over the world. I extend a very warm welcome to you sir.

We have with us Smt. Revathi. She needs no introduction. The very first song she sung for a Tamil film won her the National award. She is known for rendering the Hindola raaga in her melodious voice. Madam, all of us here are eagerly waiting for you to sing the famous Hindola composition.

We have Smt. Mangala with us. Mangala madam is Prof Alok's Kannada teacher. She will be launching the book. Madam, Prof. Alok was very particular that you should attend this event. On behalf of Prof. Alok I extend a very warm welcome to you. I thank Smt. Vasundhara Alok and her parents, who have graced this occasion. I welcome each and every booklovers.

.....Thank you all"

Dr. Rao stood up and started. He said;

"I am very happy to attend this function. When the organizers approached me to speak on this occasion, I gave my consent because of these two people. This is an occasion to express my deep gratitude to Prof. Alok and Smt. Revathi.

My daughter-in-law, was widowed when my son met with a car accident in New York. My daughter-in-law did not speak a word for two to three months. She used to find solace in listening to the alaaps sung by this great lady. She booked tickets for me and my wife to attend Smt. Revathi's concert in Chennai. I was so much overpowered by the divine melody of her voice that I waited for her to get a few moments to talk to her. When I went to express my sincere feelings of happiness, she promised to come to my house and talk to my daughter-in- law. In spite of her busy schedule, she came to my house, met my daughter- in- law and talked to her. I could see real happiness radiating from my daughter-in-law. Revathi, I am indeed grateful to you.

Prof. Alok had come to me to make some notes for some of his lectures on the Kannada poems of the Navodaya period. Being a professor of English, he had an in-depth knowledge of the romantic era of English poetry. When he had recorded his commentaries for the songs sung by Revathi, I could understand the genius that was Alok. When the publishers sent his novel for a critical review, I read it with all interest.

Alok represents a bridge between two generations of writers. He is modern in outlook, while, at the same time, maintains respect in our traditions. He believes in freedom of thought and exercises restraint when it comes to transgression of our established values. The social frame work of India accepts the liberalized ways of modern living, but not bold enough to come out of its established value system. This conflict in the Indian society is beautifully represented by the two characters Alok and Revathi that Alok has so artistically carved out of his imagination. He has retained the same names for his characters. I presume that he has done this intentionally to provide a spontaneous flow. The story of the three brothers and their mother Gracey's story is very interesting. Sr. Clara's love for Reena (Revathi) is very touching. Vasundhara's strength lies in her ability to forgive Revathi. Alok's feeling of guilt for having had an extramarital affair and the way the two women face the crisis is remarkable. As I read through Revathi's journey to Chennai to find out her father, I was in tears. The strength of the woman, as a beacon of light to the entire mankind shows the author's level of maturity and his quality of mind. In the end the author introduces Rashmi, a woman with her firm resolve, to continue her journey in the fond memory of her husband. Although, this appears a little old fashioned to the modern mind, it cautions Revathi's temptations about the thoughts of her acceptance to Alok's sexual urges. Alok has artistically used the sea, the Hindola raaga, the malkauns alaaps to decorate the story line. The Hindola represents the changing emotions, swinging from one extreme of happiness to the other extreme of sadness. It is an undercurrent throughout the flow of the story. Vasundhara stands like a pillar of strength while forgiving her husband's act and help him come out of a complex disorder. She comes to know that Revathi's initiative to have sex with her husband was more a cry for motherhood than to derive a sexual pleasure. When Revathi comes out with a confession, she supports Revathi during her pregnancy and post pregnancy days.

Then we have Allan, who comes to know that he does not belong to the Desouza lineage and tries to serve his real father in his last days, his efforts to educate Alice… Some of these events are presented in a beautiful manner.

The author's firm belief in the supremacy of human values elevates this story to a very high level.

I have read the book as a critic and not as Alok, my friend. I wish him all the best.

Revathi's fear that Alok might have ended up the novel with Revathi consenting happily to Alok's sexual advances was removed. She thanked Alok in her mind that he had treated her with respect.

Revathi commenced her programme with a devotional hymn singing in praise of Lord Vinayaka. She sang the Hindola composition "Rama Mantrava Japiso".

When she sang "Chandramukhi prana sakhi " she spoke a few words about Alok. She said,

"It was Alok's concept to introduce the Malkauns alaaps in the beginning of the song. He explained the meaning of this song so beautifully in his baritone voice. It was that programme that made a hundred thousand hits on YouTube." Revathi informed the audience.

There was a huge round of applause.

Alok started speaking.

"After Dr. Rao's brilliant speech, I have no words to speak.

I was very particular that Mangala madam should release my book. I was perhaps in my ninth standard. I remember her sitting on the platform clad in a beautiful silk saree with veena in her hand. That was the first time I heard this song. After the class, I went to her and asked her the meaning of the song. She explained it so beautifully that it has made an indelible imprint in my memory. I was drawn to this raaga. I did not try to understand the musicology part of that raaga. It appeared as if someone was singing to me at moments of my emotional distress. When my mood swung to the other extreme of the highest state of happiness – Aananda as they call it in Samskruta, I used to sing this raaga for myself. This raaga had a profound impact on me.

I had to go to Udupi to attend to my father-in-law during his post-operative period. I opened the gate outside. As I approached the door there was this divine alaap sung by someone inside the house. I walked stealthily to gain some more time to listen to that melodious voice. I didn't know who was singing. I stood there for a few minutes. Revathi appeared when I rang the door bell. It was like an angel, who had come from the heavens to sing for me. She was singing that Malkauns alaap. My novel which was in its embryonic phase had taken its birth at that instant. The rest is history.

I was born in a highly conservative family which reflected strong traditional and moral values. My father was an idealist. He was a dreamer and loved to live in a world of his own. He belonged to the pre-independence days and was a staunch Gandhian. He put the society above family and emphasized the value of sacrifice. My mother was an antithesis of my father's views. She was strong-minded pragmatic woman. To her family was supreme and all other things came later. I saw the strength of the woman in my mother first and later in Vasundhara of my novel. I must admit that many of the incidents that occur in the novel are real life incidents that have occurred to the various characters.

In a male dominated society such as ours, woman is

a lone fighter. In some of the villages in Tamil Nadu, female babies are thrown in dustbins and sometimes burnt alive. Varadaraja, in the novel, does the sensible thing of bringing his granddaughter to the church where Fr. Bernard receives the child.

The modern woman faces a different situation where she has to maintain the equilibrium of the family. We find the modern woman working in offices, colleges, courts, hospitals… practically in every region of our life. It is her strength of mind that I have tried to portray through this novel. As Dr. Rao rightly put it, it is my firm belief in the supremacy of human values that has been projected in the novel.

Thank you."

There was a thunderous applause. Alok heaved a sense of relief.

The next day, Revathi was packing her things. Alok came to her. He asked her,

"Is the ending okay."

"It is really good. I was afraid of the end in which you had thought of renewing the affair between Alok and Revathi," Revathi said.

"That would have made them clandestine lovers. I want Vasundhara to live happily. I also want Allan and Revathi live happily with Ananya."

Just then, Allan made a dramatic entry into Alok's house.

"I was curious to know the real woman. Last night, I drove all the way from Mangalore to Bangalore.

Alok, This is a great attempt in making any one realize the importance of womanhood. Thanks for portraying me as a kind soul. … Thanks for everything."

Allan started driving. It started drizzling yet again. The cool breeze was flowing. He said

"We part now to meet again."